Alexx Andria is a *US...*
author who writes ab...
exterior but a soft, wa...
sweet but dirty roman...
of course, sizzling scenes in the bedroom (or kitchen,
or wherever they happen to end up) and a guaranteed
HEA.

If you liked *Beddable Billionaire*, why not try

Close to the Edge by Zara Cox
Getting Lucky by Avril Tremayne
Forbidden Pleasure by Taryn Leigh Taylor

Discover more at millsandboon.co.uk

BEDDABLE BILLIONAIRE

ALEXX ANDRIA

MILLS & BOON

First Published in Great Britain 2018
by Mills & Boon, an imprint of HarperCollins*Publishers*
1 London Bridge Street, London, SE1 9GF

© 2018 Kimberly Sheetz

ISBN: 978-0-263-93229-4

MIX
Paper from
responsible sources
FSC® C007454

This book is produced from independently certified FSC™ paper
to ensure responsible forest management.
For more information visit www.harpercollins.co.uk/green.

Printed and bound in Spain
by CPI, Barcelona

CHAPTER ONE

Lauren

"AND I WANT YOU, Lauren, to cover the story."

"Excuse me, I'm sorry, what?" I paused my notes to meet my editor's stare, stifling the groan that wanted to pop from my mouth. Truthfully, I was only half listening during this morning's staff meeting, but what little I'd heard wasn't exactly flipping my interest switch.

"'Hottest Bachelor in Town.' I want you to write it," Patrice answered, tapping her manicured finger against the slick tabletop. "Pay attention, please."

I didn't say the actual word, but my expression clearly said *blech*, and Patrice Winneham, executive editor of *Luxe* magazine, wasn't known for her willingness to hear objections. "Problem?" she asked with a layer of frost blanketing her tone.

The last thing I wanted to write was some frivolous article on New York's most eligible and, more important, rich bachelors, but I needed my job. "No problem," I lied through my teeth. By now it should've become second nature, but it still curdled my guts to pretend to care about stories that held no bearing on actual life.

Like the world needed another spread on complete and utter nonsense. The longer I worked for *Luxe*, the more I was certain I would be required to turn in my feminist card because of crap assignments like this.

Who knew the going rate for a piece of your soul is the bargain-basement price of rent on a shitty apartment in Brooklyn. From my peripheral I caught our newest and youngest staffer nearly wetting herself to land this gig, and I readily threw her a bone.

"Actually, I really think Daphne would kill a story like that," I suggested, casting a helpful look down the boardroom table toward the young redhead. Daphne was practically nodding her head off in eager agreement, salivating at the prospect. I smiled. "She's got that young voice that I think would really sell the piece far better than me."

Also, because the idea of pandering to an overprivileged prick is about as appealing as jamming a pen in my eye. But I couldn't exactly say that without risking my job, and as shitty as the job was, it paid the bills— granted, *barely*—but still, they were paid.

"Yes, and she's also gullible," Patrice replied without apology, continuing with a briefly held smile, "and would likely end up falling in love with the man before the interview was finished. That's a headache I don't need. No, you'll do the interview. End of story." Patrice added with a warning glower, "And wear something nice. You're representing *Luxe*."

I ignored Patrice's not-so-subtle dig. Fashion wasn't my God, and I didn't worship at the altar of haute couture. I'd wear what I pleased. "Fit before fashion" was my mantra, and I didn't feel the least bit sorry for the women who chose to trudge around the city in high heels who, by the end of the day, were rubbing the agony from their barking dogs.

Nope, I sailed right past them in my sensible flats, happy as a clam and stealing their cab because I could run faster.

I caught Daphne's crestfallen expression. Poor girl, I could only imagine how her dreams of working at a high-end magazine like *Luxe* were nothing like the reality.

I remembered being that idealistic newbie.

Now I was the jaded staffer who ran on a steady diet of cynicism and sarcasm, with the occasional sprinkling of "WTF?" thrown in for flavor.

Patrice, satisfied that her word was law, moved on with a smug smile. "We have managed to snag one of the sexiest bachelors yet from a distinguished family, old-world money, if you can imagine such a thing anymore. A real *Italian stallion*, if you will, and having this hottie on the cover is going to snag eyeballs, but I need someone experienced to handle the copy."

Irritated and bored but having at least the sense to put on a good face, I forced a smile to ask, "And the name of this sexy and single vagina hound?"

"Wait for it…" Patrice paused for dramatic effect before gushing, "Nico Donato of Donato Inc. His family hails from Italy, starting with a humble yet wildly successful winery in Tuscany. Isn't that dreamy? Does anything else scream *romance* more than the Italian countryside?"

I wouldn't know, I wanted to quip. It'd been a long time since I'd experienced anything resembling romance after my ex ran off when I was five months pregnant— six years ago.

It was safe to say the most romance I'd had in my life consisted of furtive moments spent hiding in the closet with my Magic Wand.

Was it TMI if I admitted I'd already burned through three of those hardy vibrators? I rubbed at the phantom scorch mark left over from my last vibrator when it rudely caught fire in my hand.

So, yeah, romance? Not even sure I would recognize it if it bit me in the ass, but that was okay because men were a complication I didn't need in my life. I was perfectly happy with the way things were, and I didn't need wine and roses from some man to feel complete.

Did I miss an actual warm body to cuddle with on cold nights? Yeah, but then, I could always get a dog or a cat and achieve the same effect, which I'd been seriously considering.

"Wow, I've seen pictures of Nico Donato, and he's definitely a hottie," Daphne gushed, her eyes alight with envy. "I can't imagine a woman alive who would turn him down if he asked."

I tried not to roll my eyes. Continuing my Golden Globe–worthy performance, I nodded like a good staffer and agreed with Patrice because I needed my job. "Sounds fantastic," I murmured, trying not to gag.

Daphne sighed, and I could practically see the cartoon hearts and rainbows floating around her head. Good grief, Patrice was probably right. Sending someone like Daphne to interview this *Italian stallion* would be like sending a lamb to slaughter. Daphne was probably still in that stage of her life when her bra and panties matched.

I was sporting underwear with a hole in it, and my bra was three years old.

Any seduction attempt for my benefit would end in laughter. Mine and his.

Don't get me wrong, I'm not ugly and I do *probably* (maybe) own a matching bra and panty set, but let's face it, fancy panties are uncomfortable, and these days, comfort was king.

#singlemom.

#allmymoneygoestomykid.

#myvibratordoesntjudge.

Patrice was talking again. "I don't know how this man has managed to remain single, but after this issue comes out...we might be able to do a follow-up for the engagement because someone is going to snag him up, I can guarantee it."

"Maybe he's an asshole?" I suggested, and the table erupted with nervous laughter, except Patrice, who frowned. I shrugged, just pointing out what everyone else was thinking but was too afraid to voice. "I mean, that seems like the obvious answer, right? Good-looking, rich but maybe his personality is rotten. There isn't enough money in the world to compensate for a shitty attitude."

"I'm sure he's a lovely human being," Patrice said pointedly. "And it'll be your job to make sure that comes across."

"And what if, just clarifying, he *isn't* a lovely human being?"

Patrice tapped her Montblanc pen on the polished table surface, the chipped ice in her blue eyes growing colder. "I'm sure he is," she finally answered. "And you'll do a fine job. I look forward to reading your copy."

More anxious laughter floated around the conference table. Why was I poking the bear in the designer suit? *I don't know.* Maybe I was PMSing. Maybe I was tired of writing stupid, fluff articles that did nothing but perpetuate the stereotype that all women cared about were hot men with big cocks.

Or I was PMSing.

Honestly, it could go either way.

It was now or never if I wanted to throw something serious into the ring. I stilled the sudden bouncing of my knee beneath the table and pushed forward with my own idea for the magazine.

"I was thinking we could do an article on Associate Justice Elena Kagan, maybe focus on how women still have to fight for positions historically held by men?"

The silence was not only deafening, but the disdain was actually painful.

Patrice sniffed with distaste. "This is *Luxe*, not *The Legal Review*. No one wants to read about a dusty old woman in a black robe unless she's wearing Donna Karan on the bench."

Daphne tittered and I wanted to shake some sense into the young twit, but Patrice was right. *Luxe* wasn't going to be breaking ground in the advancement of women's rights anytime soon. *Luxe* was all about designer shoes, perpetuating the harmful stereotypes that fostered unattainable body goals and kept women bitching and fighting among themselves.

God, maybe I was beginning to hate *Luxe*, or maybe I was just becoming a bitter bitch because I hadn't gotten laid in forever. Seeing as that wasn't likely to change anytime soon, I had to suck it up, smile and agree to interview Mr. Big Cock or else I could lose my ability to pay rent.

"I'll make the arrangements," I said, privately scribbling, *Sacrifice dignity and interview man-slut.* "Have you already set up the photographer?"

"All done. Jacques will be shooting the spread. We're thinking…Hamptons…beach time…crisp whites and blues."

"It'll make for good pictures," I agreed but inside I was rolling my eyes. *Like that idea hasn't been done a million times before.* "Everyone loves a hot guy on the beach," I said, parroting what I knew Patrice wanted to hear.

"That they do." Patrice nodded in wholehearted agreement as if she were relieved I'd finally agreed to pull my head from my ass. "And it's easy to sell advertising for beach-themed spreads. Anyway, you all have your assignments. Go on, go forth, *amaze* me."

As I left the conference room, Daphne attached herself to my hip, saying, "Have you seen Nico's picture? He's gorgeous. Blue eyes to die for, a body made for sin, and he's so sweet. A real charmer."

"How do you know he's sweet?" I countered, wryly amused and vastly curious. "Have you met?"

"Oh, no," Daphne admitted but added quickly, "just look at that face…he seems so sweet. You can tell from the eyes. His eyes tell a story."

"I'm sure they tell some sort of story," I agreed, resisting the urge to roll my eyes so hard they bounced from my skull. Perhaps I should burst her bubble and tell her the story of my *sweet* ex. The one who bailed on me and our son when he realized being a parent was going to be a full-time job that would likely cut into his playtime? I swallowed the urge because I wasn't into wasting energy, and I doubted Daphne would see anything but my being a salty bitch—especially if she found out who my ex was.

Instead, I said, "Sounds like trouble to me, but I'd be happy to be wrong. It's not likely, but it would be a nice surprise."

"You seriously don't want this assignment?" Daphne said, flabbergasted that I would turn my nose up at the opportunity to fawn over some rich guy. "I mean, Nico Donato is mega rich. I'm talking obscenely rich. Like golden toilets, I-wipe-my-ass-with-hundred-dollar-bills *Dubai rich*."

I smirked. "That rich, huh? Sounds like a delight." Although, why would anyone want to be that rich? Seemed like a lot of headaches. I'd rather be comfortable, not obscenely wealthy. Apparently, I was in the minority, considering present company. "Personally, I prefer actual toilet paper, but the good stuff, not the tissue paper that shreds the minute you slide it across your ass."

"Are you seriously talking about toilet paper?" Daphne stepped in front of me just as I headed for the break room to grab my yogurt. "Take me with you," she pleaded. "Please? He's the man of my dreams. I'd kill to meet him. What if he's my soul mate?"

"And that's exactly why I won't let you tag along," I said, maneuvering around her. "Trust me, I'm doing you a favor. Men like Donato are narcissists and they spread heartbreak like disease. I'll bet if I did a little digging I'd find scores of women who were used and tossed aside by this rich prick. Just because he's got a nice face—"

Daphne injected, "And body."

I exhaled in irritation as I continued. "Yes, *and*

body, doesn't mean he's not the devil." I retrieved my yogurt, adding for Daphne's sake, "You're young. When you get a little more seasoning, you'll figure out that *Dubai-rich* guys are usually the ones you want to steer clear from."

"You're not that much older than me," Daphne pointed out with a frown. "Why do you act like you're an old lady?"

Are we close to the same age? Impossible. Most days I felt a hundred.

"Because I don't think I was ever your age," I answered, popping the spoon in my mouth. "But if you must know, I've been burned before by a sweet talker, and experience breeds wisdom, you know?"

"So, because you got your heart broken you're never going to let anyone else in?"

Ick. When did this conversation turn into a Dr. Phil session? "As much as I adore this little tête-à-tête, I have work to do so…"

Daphne pouted but didn't continue to dog me to my desk (thank God), and I was able to eat my yogurt in relative peace while I did some poking around on the net about Donato.

My Google-fu was pretty decent, and with a few clicks I had pictures and background information on the youngest Donato.

Okay, so he was handsome, I'd give him that.

Yeah, those blue eyes were panty-droppers, and that body looked fairly chiseled from clay.

And Nico was *Dubai rich*, as Daphne liked to call it.

But I couldn't find any information on anything useful or worthwhile that he might've been associated with.

No philanthropy.

No peace work.

No good deeds on record.

However, I did find some paparazzi photos of Nico doing body shots off the belly of a hot-bodied coed during spring break at Lake Havasu.

Yep. I took another bite. *Total douchebag.* Life was so unfair. How did guys like Nico always get ahead when hardworking people, like myself, had to struggle and scrape for every dime?

I wallowed in a moment of self-pity before sighing and printing out the relevant information I would need for my fluff article.

"I love my job," I murmured to myself. "I love my job." To ground my motivation more firmly, I glanced at the picture of my son on my desk. Grady's gap-toothed smile was all the motivation I needed to shut my mouth, put my head down and get the job done.

Houston Beaumont was a useless human being, but our son was the light of my life and I couldn't regret deciding to cancel the adoption paperwork.

Grady wasn't planned—hell, my relationship, if you can call it that, with Houston hadn't been planned either—but I'd do anything for that cute little dirty-blond imp who called me Mama.

And I thanked my lucky stars every day that Houston hadn't tried to sue for custody. He'd been more than happy to forget all about me and his son.

I didn't mind being a single mom if it meant knowing that Grady didn't have to be shuttled between two different worlds—mine and his father's.

Drawing a deep breath, I nodded to myself, girding

my loins, so to speak, so I could swallow my dignity without choking.

I could do this. No sweat.

At least one thing was for certain—there was no way Donato was going to charm the pants off me—a fact he would discover right away if he was dumb enough to try.

CHAPTER TWO

Nico

"NICE TO MEET YOU, Mr. Donato. Lauren Hughes, *Luxe* magazine."

The tall brunette thrust her hand toward me as if she were a man—strong, no-nonsense, obligatory—her deep brown eyes the only feature worth noting if I were to go off first impressions.

The handshake lasted all of two seconds, no lingering, and then she was sitting primly at the farthest point on the sofa in my living room, recorder in hand, expression blandly expectant, as if preparing to mentally vacate as soon as I started talking.

"Pleasure to meet you, Miss Hughes," I said, my gaze quickly taking in the shape-swallowing shift dress that completely obscured her figure and the functional flats that finished off the wretched ensemble. I think my maid dressed better than this woman. "I hope the traffic wasn't too heavy."

"Dealing with traffic is just one of those things you get used to when you live in New York," she said with a brief smile. The look in her eyes told me she wasn't one for small talk, which suited me fine because I hated it, too—but I was definitely not quite sure what to make of this stiff-as-a-board reporter.

Definitely not what I was expecting, and I was fucking disappointed. Where was the hot chick in the curve-hugging pencil skirt, glasses sitting demurely on the bridge of her nose, hair upswept in a delicate yet artfully messy bun? *Not sitting on my sofa, that's for sure.*

"Have you always been a New Yorker?" she asked with a direct stare. No makeup that I could tell. Not even a hint of mascara to brighten up her eyes. A pity. Those dark eyes with a little assistance might even be pretty. "My editor tells me that your family is from Italy, originally."

"Yes, so the legend says," I answered, trying for a little wry humor. When she didn't so much as offer a polite chuckle, I cleared my throat and followed with, "Tuscany, actually, but we've been in New York for two generations now. Our Italian roots are fairly weak at this point. All I inherited from my Italian ancestors is a love of fine women, wine and pasta."

"Ah."

"Your skin tone is beautiful. Are you Latina?" Was she Latina? Or perhaps Native American? Maybe even Creole?

"A hodgepodge of nationalities," she answered, adjusting herself on the sofa. "Just lucked out in the skin department, I guess. So, tell me, how does it feel to be named one of New York's most eligible bachelors?"

"Well, you know the saying, the only thing worse than being talked about is not being talked about," I said with a wink. "But it should be interesting to see what crawls out of the woodwork once the magazine hits the stands. I'm always down for an adventure."

"If you're not interested in finding love, you could've turned down the interview," she said, again with that brief smile that I was beginning to suspect was patronizing. "I'm sure we could've found someone who was more aligned with the purpose of the spread."

"Who said I'm not looking for love?"

"Well, I mean, it was kind of implied by your earlier statement. To call the women who might be interested as things that 'crawl out of the woodwork' sounds insulting, don't you think?"

Annoyance threatened to color my tone as I admitted, "That was a poor choice of words. Maybe I'm more embarrassed by the attention than I like to let on. The truth is, I've never considered myself interesting enough for an entire magazine spread, and I'm not quite sure how I was selected."

False humility was always good for a few grace points, but I think Lauren saw right through my attempt, which, in itself, threw off my game.

Hell, everything about this woman threw me.

I'd thought *Luxe* might've sent one of their show ponies to interview me. Maybe an intern with a tight body, perky tits and an ass that would put a gymnast to shame; or, a more sophisticated staffer with legs for days and long blond hair, perfect for a man's fist to wrap around to guide a hot mouth onto a ready cock.

I bit back my growing disappointment. No nubile intern; no savvy staffer. *Luxe* had sent *her*.

The dour killjoy.

Was that a coffee stain on her dress?

And that austere bun squatting on top of her head was tight enough to give her a poor man's face-lift.

"So...you work at Luxe?" I asked, sinking into the sofa, regarding her curiously. Perhaps she was a free-lance writer...

"Three years now," Lauren answered with a short smile before moving on. "I can appreciate how busy you are, so thank you for agreeing to this interview. My editor, Patrice, was excited to have one of the hottest bachelors in the city as the center feature."

Funny how her words said one thing but her tone said something completely different. This was starting off as the weirdest interview I'd ever granted. Didn't she realize I was a catch? That there were scores of women who wanted to be on this sofa with me? *Beneath me, specifically.* Frankly, on a hotness scale of one to ten, she was reaching for a four; *she* ought to be the one *excited* to be interviewing me.

But she didn't look tickled or impressed. Or even happy to be there. Was that a tick of boredom in those chocolate eyes?

My male pride demanded a better response. I couldn't have a four turning her nose up at me. Maybe I just needed to warm her up.

"Tell me about yourself," I suggested with a charming smile, the one that never failed to soften even the most rigid of women. "Do you enjoy working for *Luxe*?"

"Not here to interview me," she said with a wag of her finger like a schoolmarm. "We're here to talk about you."

"I like to get to know the people who are interviewing me," I returned, lobbing the ball back into her court, which she let drop with an unsatisfying *splat* when she remained silent, her fake, professional smile firmly in place. "Nothing? Hmm…have we met before?" I asked, half wondering if I'd slept with her at some point and forgotten to call her afterward. I mean, I couldn't see myself purposefully sleeping with a four, but if vodka was involved…anything was possible.

"Not likely," Lauren answered, puzzled by my question, and frankly, I was a little relieved until she said, "I doubt we run in the same circles," and it was that tiny undercurrent of condescension that narrowed my gaze.

"It just seems that maybe we've met before and perhaps I made a bad impression…"

"Not at all," she assured me, but her gaze remained unimpressed and flatly disinterested with anything that came out of my mouth, as if she were doing penance for a crime in a past life. Did I smell or something? I shifted against the unfamiliar sense of disdain emanating from the woman. "So, just tell me what you'd like the people to know about Nico Donato," she suggested as if being helpful. "Charities you support, hobbies, what you do to make the world a better place?"

Suddenly, everything clicked. I saw her game now. It all made sense. The frumpy clothes, the sour attitude, the barely concealed contempt…and now the leading question that she was fairly certain she knew the answer to…all meant to paint me into a corner of her choosing.

Lauren Hughes wasn't here to give me a fair shake; she was here to judge me. Time to make things interesting. If she thought she had me figured out, I'd give her something meaty to chew on. I grinned, sharing, "Actually, I don't mean to brag but last week, I paid all the alcohol tabs at Buxom. Probably spent close to ten grand on that bill, but I was happy to do it. That's just me…always giving."

"Buxom…the strip club?" she repeated, her expression screwing into a frown.

"It's more of a gentleman's club, but yeah, I suppose you could call it a strip club, but you know, those girls work so hard. It's really a misunderstood profession. I'm sure at least one of those ladies is working to put herself through law school, and how can you not support higher education, right?"

"Very generous of you," Lauren returned drily, her lips pursing a little before saying, "It must be very nice to be able to fund other people's vices."

"Vice is fun, you should try it sometime."

"Thanks but I think I'm good."

"Oh, come now, surely there's something taboo that flips your switch."

"Sorry, pretty boring."

That I can believe. But for the sake of argument, I said, "Indulge me," my interest in the interview taking a hard left in a different direction. I wanted to see how ruffled I could make Little Miss Sourpuss's feathers. "Perhaps…you enjoy a little spanking now and then? A little 'tie me up, tie me down' action behind closed doors?"

A flush climbed her throat to stain her cheeks as she shut me down. "Not really," she answered, gesturing with professional courtesy to the recorder in her hand even as I sensed I'd gotten under her skin. "Shall we return to the interview, please?"

"Oh? Isn't that what we were doing?"

"I can't put in the article that you frequent Buxom.

It's not the most savory bit of information for an article trying to make you sound like a catch."

"I am a catch."

She shrugged as if to say, *we can agree to disagree*, but suggested, "Let's get back to basics. I have some tried-and-true questions that usually lead to good, safe answers. Shall we?"

Sounds boring as hell. "Lead on."

"Puppies or kittens?"

"Neither. They both shed, vomit and shit all over the place." I gestured to my penthouse suite. "Clearly, I value a clean space in which to entertain."

"Hmm...do you like any sort of pet?"

I considered her question, but I really couldn't think of anything. Living things were too much work. Unfortunately, I learned that the hard way when I was seven. *RIP, poor Bubbles the goldfish.* "No, not really."

"Nothing?" she pressed, as incredulous as if I'd admitted I enjoy tripping old people in my spare time. "Not even a hamster or a rabbit?"

I smiled, wondering how far I could push Miss Hughes's boundaries. I wasn't above playing dirty either—because dirty was fun. I drew a breath as if in thought, then said, "I do enjoy games."

"Oh? Like board games? Clue, Monopoly, that sort of thing?" she asked, cocking her head with curiosity. "Or like card games?"

"Have you ever heard of pony play?"

Her expression screwed into a cute mask of confusion. "Pony play? Like polo or something?"

I chuckled, enjoying this way more than I should, but I was hungry for that sudden blush that would follow my explanation. For a brief—and I'm talking nanosecond brief—moment, when the high color brightened her cheeks, she was almost pretty.

And I was curious just how far I could push.

I started to explain, using my hands for illustration. "Imagine a beautiful mane attached to a short, notched column and then imagine that column going straight up a lovely ass, held in place by the cheeks, then you fit your sweet horsey with a halter and a bit and if you're lucky, you get to ride her all night."

She gasped in shock, thrown off her game. Flustered, she shut off her recorder, shooting me a dark, exasperated look, but those cheeks were so hot I could fry an egg.

And holy fuck, miracle of miracles, she'd just rocketed past a level four and hit a solid seven.

"Mr. Donato...that...that...that's *disgusting*."

I laughed. "Don't knock it till you try it."

"And inappropriate. Like, *really* inappropriate for the purposes of this interview. I can't go writing that you like to stick things up women's asses and ride them like horses. I mean, c'mon!"

I pretended to be perplexed. "I thought you wanted something authentic. This is the real me. I believe my potential mate should share my open-minded views on sex. Otherwise we're not going to make it. I'd rather be honest and up-front from the start, don't you think? Imagine all the pain and heartache we'd both suffer if I wasn't honest and then when we discover we're incompatible sexually, it's nothing but tears and accusations. I've seen it too many times. Honesty is the best policy when it comes to sex. If you haven't learned that yet, you will."

I'd caught her neatly with seemingly earnest logic, and there wasn't much she could say to refute my point.

Lauren pursed her lips as if holding back what she really wanted to say. *Go ahead girl, let loose. Tell me what a perverted dick I am.* I wanted to push all her buttons. "Mr. Donato—"

"Please call me Nico. *Mr. Donato* is so formal and boring. Besides, when I hear Mr. Donato, I immediately look for my oldest brother, Luca, or my father—both are giant killjoys, if you know what I mean, and I'm nothing like either of them." I settled my gaze on her with intrigue and fluttered my fingers suggestively as I followed with, "Tell me, what taboo sexual act gets you all revved up? Surely, there's something that gets the home fires burning…"

But instead of taking the bait, she narrowed her gaze and shut me down with a hard "May I speak frankly?"

This ought to be interesting. I gestured with magnanimous flourish. "Please do."

"I know you have a reputation for being a playboy—"

"I have a reputation?" I repeated, pretending to be concerned. "Tell me…are they talking about my cock? Pardon my bluntness, but if they are saying it's anything less than a full eight inches, they are lying through their damn teeth."

Lauren ignored my provocative statement and pushed forward, saying, "Your reputation as a Lothario precedes you, Mr. Donato," deliberately using my formal title rather than my name. "But I'm here to interview you as an eligible bachelor—an interview you agreed to, if I may remind you, so if you wouldn't mind at least pretending to take this seriously, we can finish with the interview and I'll be on my way. How does that sound?"

Now it was my turn to be annoyed. What would it take to knock loose the stick wedged up her ass? Even as she was determined to keep me at arm's length and locked out, the subtle widening of her eyes gave away more than she knew—and that fired up my need for more.

"How about dinner, tonight?" I proposed, imagining what she might look like if her hair wasn't pulled to the back of her skull like a nun's visiting the pope.

"No, thank you," she answered, pursing her lips with irritation. "The interview, please."

Such a dogged sense of duty. I released a sigh and leaned back, motioning for her to continue. "Fine. I'll answer your questions but only if you'll answer mine."

"That's not how this works." Exasperation colored her voice but not to the level I imagined she was feeling. If I were a betting man, I'd say Lauren Hughes wanted to hog-tie me, land a swift kick to my nuts and stuff my silk tie down my throat.

Not the usual response I received from women.

And, fuck me, I liked it.

The game we were playing had just leveled up.

CHAPTER THREE

Lauren

I PINNED NICO with a pointed gaze, my patience at its thinnest, realizing that my instincts were correct and that this interview was a waste of my time. Patrice could find a different person to dance in circles with this egomaniac. "I'm not here to play games. If you'd like to reschedule for when you're feeling less like an immature jerk, please let me know." I rose and shouldered my purse, ready to leave.

"Hold up," Nico said, managing to hustle fast enough to catch me before I walked out the door. "I'm sorry. What can I say? I'm an immature jerk at times. Would you believe you make me nervous? Can we start over?"

I make *him* nervous? I wasn't sure I bought that line, but there was something vaguely earnest about his statement that made me pause. If I could salvage this interview, it would work in my favor, but there was something about Nico that set my teeth on edge. Still, my life would be ten times easier if I could manage to get this story filed, and I couldn't do that without his interview. I blew out a short breath before relenting with a wary, "You promise to behave?"

His blue eyes sparkled with mischief, but he managed a very solemn "Scout's honor"—which was laughable in itself but at least he'd tried to apologize, right? I supposed I could give him another chance.

"I sincerely doubt you've ever been a Scout in your life," I murmured, settling on the sofa again; but when he joined me on the same sofa, I narrowed my gaze, suspicious all over again. "Wouldn't you be more comfortable over there?" I motioned to his previous seat.

"Actually," he said with mild embarrassment, "I have a hard time hearing in my left ear—sailing accident when I was a kid—so in all seriousness, if we're going to do this, I need to sit a bit more closely."

I felt a bit sheepish as my mouth shaped an embarrassed moue and nodded. "Okay, then." Nico waited patiently while I fished my recorder from my purse, ready to start again. "Describe your perfect date," I proposed, thrusting the recorder toward Nico with an expectant expression.

He didn't hesitate. "Sex. Dirty, sexy, sweaty sex."

Oh, good grief. Was it too much to ask to get a PG-13 answer from the man? "Can you perhaps give me *something* to work with? I can't write that all it takes to make a perfect date in your book is lots of sex."

"Why not? It's the truth," he said, and this time I could tell he was being completely honest. I stiffened against the unwelcome and inappropriate thrill that chased my spine as he added, "It's the best way to get to know someone."

I hesitated, trying to decide which way to proceed. My gut said to pack up and leave, but I was genuinely curious as to why he believed in his answer. *Curios-*

ity killed the cat, remember? And yet, I challenged for the sake of argument, "Seriously? Pardon me if I call bullshit. Don't you find that just a little shallow?"

"Not at all," he said, enjoying the chance to defend his answer. "What's a date all about? Getting to know someone, right?"

I took the bait and nodded slowly, remaining wary. "Yes, I suppose so."

He smiled, asking, "May I?" reaching for my hand. I hesitated but relented, allowing Nico to grasp my free hand. He flipped my hand, palm-side down, to trace the small veins beneath my skin. I fought to keep the shivers at bay, trying to remain outwardly unaffected, even bored. "Let's say the underside of your palm represents your private self and the top of your hand represents the shield we put up to protect the soft parts of our hand that we only trust with those we know won't hurt us."

"Okay," I said, puzzled, drawing a short breath as my heart rate quickened. "How does that relate to sex on the first date?"

"I challenge you to tell me any other way to truly get to know someone without using sex." He slowly rotated my hand so my palm faced up. "Sex reveals vulnerabilities, our deep truths, and strips away the facades that we readily wear to hide ourselves from the world. In other words, sex removes the shield, leaving us with our soft spots unprotected."

I swallowed as tiny trembles I couldn't contain shook my body. I pressed my lips together before my tongue darted to wet my bottom lip. Suddenly, it was very warm in his apartment, and the air had become charged with electricity. "I…guess I see your point…

but it's a stretch," I lied, loathe to let him see how his little demonstration had turned up my internal heat.

He laughed, disagreeing. "In truth, Miss Hughes... sex is the great equalizer, and what better way to determine whether or not you are a match than when you are in your deepest reality?"

I allowed him to hold my hand a moment longer than necessary, then quickly withdrew, shaking my head with a wobbly "Interesting theory but I'm not sure I can put that in the article. *Luxe* isn't that kind of magazine. We're more about classy, not trashy."

I was totally lying. Patrice would eat that shit up and probably highlight the passage in a glitzy pull quote, but I couldn't bring myself to admit that.

The awful truth was, Nico had somehow turned a far-fetched explanation into the sexiest demonstration I'd ever experienced, and I hated the way I felt way too breathless for my own comfort. I wasn't like Daphne, easily seduced or beguiled with a few choice words, but I could still feel the phantom touch of his fingers tracing my skin.

Nico didn't seem to mind and shrugged. "I'm only being honest. You asked what my idea of a perfect date would be, and I answered you."

I rubbed at my hand. "So lie to me," I quipped with a flustered laugh, realizing my gaffe, then amended quickly, "I mean, don't lie but maybe use your imagination. You have to remember that women are going to read this and want to know how they can impress you. This is your chance to put your dreams out there."

"As in my dream woman?" he asked for clarification, shaking his head, as if he knew there was no such thing. Something about that fatalistic opinion struck me as sad, though I wasn't a hopeless romantic by any means. I knew that true love was just a greeting card sentiment, but a part of me wished it were real. Maybe deep down, Nico did, too.

"Sure," I answered, curious as to what he considered the epitome of a female partner.

But Nico didn't seem interested in following that plot thread and detoured neatly as his gaze traveled the angle of my neck as sensuously as if his lips were nibbling a trail. "Were you ever a dancer?" he surprised me by asking.

My cheeks flushed with heat as I admitted, "Uh, yes, when I was younger. A long time ago."

"But you're not anymore."

"No."

"Why'd you give it up?"

Even though my hopeful ballet career died a long time ago, it still hurt to revisit those memories. I should've snapped my mouth shut but I didn't. "I hurt my knee performing a *grand jeté* when I was sixteen. It was never the same afterward and I knew I'd never make it to the New York City Ballet with that kind of injury, so I quit dancing altogether."

"Tragic," he murmured, and I sensed he was being genuine. His expression turned quizzical. "From what I understand, injuries are common for dancers but many heal with the right care and therapy. Why didn't you?"

Nico could never possibly understand how something like that would've been totally outside of my family's capabilities financially. I'd known the minute the muscle had torn that my career was done. "My parents didn't have the money for the intensive care that my injury required to put me back to where I was," I explained, stiffening against the inevitable ache in my heart for what would never be. "I wasn't going to ask my parents to bankrupt themselves so I could continue dancing." The clip in my tone was a warning that he was treading on dangerous ground. I lifted the recorder with a pointed look. "Now, about that dream woman..."

Nico smiled, slow and easy, ignoring my lead. "I've always had a thing for dancers. There's just something about the graceful way they carry themselves that always seems to stick with them, even long after they've stopped dancing."

I couldn't argue. I prided myself on maintaining proper posture, a throwback to my dancing days. An imaginary string pulled taut perpetually suspended my head. I could still hear my dance instructor's voice, *"Backs straight, chins high, dahling!"*

"Do you miss dancing?" he asked, interrupting my short reverie.

I exhaled a long breath. "It was a long time ago."

"That's not an answer," he chided.

"I'm not the one being interviewed."

His gaze inadvertently dipped to my dress, and I could practically feel his judgment, same as when Patrice openly curled her lip at my fashion choices. I lifted my chin and met his gaze squarely, almost daring him to make a comment so I could shoot him down. *I swear, don't people have better things to do than judge what other people are wearing? Is the world really that shallow?* Of course it was... I worked for a fashion magazine and I saw it firsthand.

Nico surprised me when he pulled away, his gaze narrowing as if he'd heard my internal dialogue. "Let's get down to brass tacks. You don't like me very much," he stated matter-of-factly. "Why?"

My cheeks flushed with guilt. I really needed to work on my poker skills if he saw through me so easily. Or maybe I hadn't really tried all that hard to disguise my contempt. Either way, my inability to smother what I was thinking or feeling had just bitten me in the ass—again.

"I like you just fine," I protested, trying for an earnest expression, but I felt as if I probably looked like the Joker with a pasted-on smile so I tried a different tack. "I mean, fine enough to do this interview. I doubt we have enough in common to enjoy a friendship, but other than that...I'm sure you're great."

"You're a terrible liar," he said, enjoying my sudden squirming. "Why don't you like me?"

He wasn't going to stop pressing. I could lay it all on the line and risk everything or I could try to lie through my teeth and maybe flirt a little. The latter made my dignity shrivel like a raisin, so that left me with pure honesty. I shut off the recorder—again. "Not that it matters for the sake of this interview, but maybe, I don't care for your *personality* type."

"Which is?"

I waved away his question. "Are we really doing this? Look, I'm sure there are plenty of women who would give their right foot to date you, I'm just not one of them."

"I didn't ask if you wanted to *date* me, I asked why you didn't *like* me. But since you brought it up, why wouldn't you want to date me?"

I hesitated, wondering how I'd lost control of this interview. I should've realized the Donatos were master manipulators. I should've been more diligent—or walked out when I'd had the chance.

But my chance to right the ship had just sailed.

Nico snorted with derision. "C'mon, you really think I can't smell your condescension from a mile away? Sweetheart, you're going to have to be a better actress than that if you're going to fool anyone into believing that you don't think I'm a big pile of shit." I opened my mouth to protest, but he wasn't finished. "What I don't understand is why *Luxe* would insult my family in such a manner as to send someone who clearly hates me to do this interview. I mean, what the fuck? Was this all a joke or something?"

Just apologize and appease his monster-sized ego. The answer seemed so simple, and yet I couldn't do it. I stiffened, wary. "If you planned on being a dick from the start, why didn't you let me leave?"

He shrugged. "I was curious but now I'm just bored and irritated."

"Why should my opinion matter at all?" I countered, feeling reckless. There was something about Nico that I couldn't quite shake, something that made me want to push when otherwise I might wisely fold.

Or maybe I was just tired of being railroaded for the sake of a paycheck. Patrice had never been my biggest fan, and this colossal train wreck of an interview shouldn't come as too big of a surprise, right?

Would she fire me?

Maybe?

Nico leaned forward, invading my space. "You think I'm another useless trust-fund baby with nothing better to do than spend my money on hookers and blow or at the very least strippers and booze." When I didn't deny it, he barked a laugh at my expense, as if I were an unprepared newb who hadn't done a lick of research. "My family donates gobs of money to various organizations and charities, but it is scattered among the different companies we own. We choose not to advertise our philanthropic endeavors because we believe that's private and we aren't looking for accolades. So we don't talk much about those things, but because we don't advertise, you make an assumption that I'm just another rich playboy who wipes his ass with money."

I had thought all of those things. Had I underestimated him? Was it possible? Right now I felt like an embittered, snarky bitch who hated all men, and it wasn't a nice feeling at all. "I may have misjudged you on first appearances," I admitted in a low tone, "but you haven't done much to disabuse me of my first impression."

"Was I supposed to? Or were you supposed to come here with an open mind?"

I swallowed, squarely put into my place by the most unlikely of people.

"You were rude," he stated flatly.

I chewed the side of my cheek before uttering a reluctant "Yes."

"You admit it?"

I'd have rather swallowed knives but nodded. "I didn't realize I was being so rude. Please let me start over."

"I should probably just ask for another reporter. Might be for the best."

"Please don't."

"I think it would be better for everyone involved."

"I assure you, it's not. Unless you want an idiot writing your article," I ground out. For someone who was supposed to be groveling, I was terrible at it.

"Nobody likes to be judged," he said quietly, and I understood where he was coming from. I suppose not even Nico Donato was free from judgment, though I never imagined that he might care what others thought.

"I'm sorry," I said again, meaning it this time. "I shouldn't have come in with a preconceived idea of who you were." Nico appeared mollified enough to accept my apology. I drew a deep breath and tried a real smile. "Can we start over? Wipe the slate clean? I promise you, even though I might've started with a bad attitude, I'm a pretty good writer. No one else at *Luxe* will do as good a job as me."

Nico regarded me with speculation, his blue eyes deepening a shade. As much as I wanted to ignore the obvious, Nico Donato was easy on the eyes, and it'd been a long time since I'd allowed a man to enter my thoughts in any sort of sexual way.

Raw energy pulsed between us, parching my throat and leaving me out of sorts. Patching things between us might save my job, but I feared something far more frightening than job hunting in New York with a near-useless degree.

Nico had a thing about him…some kind of sexual voodoo, and I could already feel something happening between us even if it was in fits and starts—but it took only a spark to burn down a forest.

And that was the part that worried me.

CHAPTER FOUR

Nico

"I'M REALLY NOT an asshole," I insisted, but I couldn't quite prevent the tiny half smile curving my mouth. Even I couldn't make that statement with a straight face, but the fact that she handled my curveball without missing a beat was arousing as fuck. I had to know more about this woman—by any means possible. "Okay, how about this... I will answer any question you have for me...over dinner."

"Dinner," she repeated with open suspicion. "Why dinner?"

"Let's be honest...we both bungled this interview. Let's wipe the slate clean and start fresh. I'm willing to believe that we're both reasonable human beings, so why not forget this terrible first impression happened and start over. Preferably over a glass of wine."

Her gaze narrowed, but the tiny smile playing at the corners of her mouth told me she enjoyed negotiating as much as I did. *Oh, the things people reveal without realizing it.* "Dinner, no wine. Purely business. No funny business," she countered, her gaze glittering as she tacked on, "at a well-lit restaurant."

I shook my head. "Here."

"I'd rather a restaurant."

I knew if I pushed, she'd push back. She wasn't the kind of woman who was easily impressed or intimidated, so I had to try something else. "May I be completely honest?" I asked. She nodded slowly, curious. "It may come as a surprise, but I love to cook. It's the one thing that I wasn't given simply because of who I am. I've earned my skills through plenty of trial and error. If I'm going to have a shot of changing your perception of me, cooking you a meal is the best way I know how."

Her stunned silence was more telling than she knew. What she couldn't know was that I was being completely honest. I felt most comfortable in the kitchen, and I took great pride in knowing that every skill I had with food was 100 percent legit. Of course, I withheld the mention that I'd discovered long ago that women found men who can cook irresistible. I couldn't count how many panties had dropped over a seemingly innocent homemade dish of *risotto alla Milanese* paired with a perfectly roasted leg of lamb.

After a long, contemplative pause, Lauren nodded, accepting my proposal. "You have yourself a clean slate, Mr. Donato. I'll see you tonight. Seven o'clock," she said, rising as she thrust her hand toward me to seal the deal. I chuckled and accepted the handshake when I really wanted to brush my lips across that pale, soft skin to watch the goose bumps cause an all-out riot. I wanted to know what stole Lauren's breath and caused those beautiful dark eyes to darken further—and I definitely wanted to know what she was hiding beneath that ugly dress. However, I played the part of the gentleman, opening her door and watching her leave without a further suggestive remark or inappropriate suggestion.

Pretty proud of myself, actually. I rarely denied myself whatever pleasure caught my eye, but I suspected Lauren was a diamond hidden inside that crusty coal and I was more interested in discovering how to reveal what I was truly interested in.

The question was, what about Lauren turned my clock? Hell, I hadn't a clue. Generally speaking, I preferred women to be soft and malleable, maybe even a little on the vapid side. But then, I wasn't accustomed to women actively pushing me away. Usually it was the other way around. Most times I had to shake the women off with a stick.

Got quite annoying, actually.

But not Lauren.

Her employment with *Luxe* came to mind, as she clearly didn't fit the blueprint for the self-indulgent magazine.

Hence, the plot thickens, eh?

Everything about the woman intrigued me, and for fuck's sake, I was bored enough to dig into the mystery.

CHAPTER FIVE

Lauren

I COULDN'T EXPLAIN what had happened between Nico and me. I'm not entirely sure how he'd managed to turn the tables so neatly, but I had to give the man props for style and finesse.

For all his talk about wanting a fresh start to make a better impression, I wasn't buying into his story, but there was something about Nico that made me want to play the game.

Was this how it started? There was a saying, "bad judgment made for good stories," and it certainly applied to my current situation. I should've shut him down, told Patrice that Donato wasn't a good fit for the center feature and moved on. But somewhere between being completely annoyed and defensive to the point where he actually had me anticipating a countermove, my interest level had changed.

I had no doubt he was playing a game with me, but I wasn't without my own skills. If he thought he could charm the pants off me with an impressive culinary show, he was headed for an aching case of blue balls, but I wasn't above enjoying a fine home-cooked meal on someone else's dime and effort.

My ex had come from a wealthy family, and Houston had pulled out all the stops to impress me. Unfortunately, it'd worked on a naive girl, but I wasn't that girl anymore. Getting knocked up and abandoned did a lot to make a girl grow up.

When I'd met Houston, I'd been just out of college, and much more trusting.

Now I was fairly certain everyone had an agenda.

Except my sweet son.

Oh, crud. Speaking of, I'd have to find a babysitter for Grady tonight. I didn't want to call my mom because she'd ask questions, but the last time I left Grady with my best friend, Ronnie, he'd gotten Grady hooked on *Drag Race*. It'd taken weeks to convince Grady that a feather boa was *not* an acceptable choice for kindergarten attire. I mean, don't get me wrong, I loved that Grady was exposed to different lifestyles and completely open to alternative ways to be a human being. But I had a hard enough time as it was with the school administrator each time Grady said or did something that shocked the pants off his teacher.

I called my younger sister, Claire, hoping that she was available. Voice mail.

I chewed my bottom lip, vacillating between calling my mom and calling Ronnie.

I went with Ronnie.

"Hey, babe, you available to watch Grady tonight for me?" I asked, hailing a cab.

"Oh, honey child, why do you do this to me? You know I would die to watch the little man, but I totally have plans already. Unless you don't mind if I take him with me," he answered with a dubious tone that immediately set off alarm bells.

"Where are you going?" I asked, wary. "No drag shows."

"Oh, poo. Well, if you're going to be like that, then no, I already have plans."

I laughed, shaking my head. "You know you can't take Grady to a drag show. Most are held at a bar."

"Don't be ridiculous. This is a private show, and mostly kid-friendly. I think."

Yeah, I wasn't about to take the chance. "Not this time," I said, chuckling. It wasn't that I didn't trust Grady to be safe with Ronnie, but sometimes my friend didn't think about how impressionable a six-year-old was, and learning how to effectively tuck a penis wasn't a skill set I needed my son to pick up anytime soon. "No worries. Enjoy your show," I said and clicked off.

That left my mom.

Ugh. My mom and I were often on opposite sides of everything. For example, my mom thought I ought to be going after Grady's dad for child support even though I'd explained that it was better for Grady and me if Houston wasn't involved. I wasn't about to poke the sleeping bear. Houston was content to pretend that he didn't have a son, and I was totally fine with that. But my mom saw only the potential dollar signs floating out the window.

"He needs to take responsibility for his son," she'd said during one of the many pointless arguments on the subject. "He has enough money—he needs to pay up."

"I don't want Houston around Grady," I'd replied,

hoping the conversation was finished. "We're better off. Houston isn't exactly ready to be a father."

"You should've thought of that before getting knocked up," Ellen Hughes disparaged with a cool look. "If your father were alive today…well, let's just say he'd be having words with that young man."

I winced, hating when she brought up the subject of my dad. "Leave Dad out of this," I warned. "The man has earned his rest after being married to you for thirty years." It was harsh, but things tended to slip out when I argued with my mother.

"Lauren Elizabeth Hughes, you watch your mouth. I didn't raise you to be disrespectful." My mother's mouth pinched as she added disapprovingly, "A boy needs his father."

"No, he doesn't if that father is a useless playboy who cares more about partying than raising a child," I returned sharply, giving my mother "the look" as I finished putting away Grady's toys. My mother took the hint and gathered her things to leave. "Do you need me to call a cab?" I asked helpfully, but my mom was already out the door.

So, yeah, I wasn't super excited to have her babysit.

I could always bring Grady with me.

The thought popped into my head almost as a joke, but then I realized maybe that was an excellent idea.

I doubted Nico would try anything inappropriate with a six-year-old boy in attendance.

Maybe I was risking my mom card for using my kid as a shield, but the idea had merit. The more I thought about it, the more I realized it was a viable solution to a sticky issue.

With Grady there, I could keep the conversation on

point and I could also use Grady as a legitimate reason to leave on time.

I'd get my interview and escape with my integrity.
Problem solved.

CHAPTER SIX

Nico

IN PREPARATION FOR TONIGHT, I had the best mood music set, soft lighting and a menu course that never failed to impress.

My buddies never failed to give me shit about my enjoyment of cooking, but I took pride in my work.

I believed men should be able to do two things well: cook and fuck.

And I excelled at both.

My doorbell went off, and I smiled at her punctuality.

I strode to the door with a wide smile, ready to go another round with Miss Hughes, but when I opened the door I stopped short, my smile freezing in place as confusion rapidly set in.

"Hello, my name is Grady." A small boy with glasses perched on his button nose thrust his little hand up at me. I faltered, inelegantly surprised by the unexpected plus-one, but Lauren filled in the blanks quickly—and, if I wasn't mistaken, I caught a spark of mischief in her dark eyes.

"Single mom, no babysitter so that means it's take-your-kid-to-work night. I hope you don't mind." She smiled broadly as if she knew throwing a kid in the mix had just crumpled all of my elaborate plans. Just then, a sexy song came on the playlist and I felt as exposed as if she'd caught me with my pants down.

Hot damn, she'd just taken things to the next level.

But I was nothing if not quick on my feet and recovered with a smile. "No worries, nice to meet you, little man," I said. I shook the boy's hand, impressed with his solid handshake. "Come in. You're in luck that I didn't plan for the lobster soufflé. I thought I might go with something a little less stuffy for our interview. I hope you like spaghetti."

Grady answered first, piping in, "I love *pasketti*. It's my favorite, but are you going to make garlic bread, too?"

Precocious little kid. I liked him already. "Of course," I answered. "Have you ever known a self-respecting Italian to serve a meal without bread?"

"Good man," Grady said, nodding with approval as he made his way into my living room, taking in the surroundings. "My mom says that you're a rich man with poor morals, but how good are you in the kitchen?"

Lauren gasped, embarrassed by her son's honesty. "Grady! Oh my goodness, I'm so sorry," she exclaimed, sending Grady a look that said, *cool it, kid*, but a smile pulled at my mouth. If I had a quarter for every time I'd embarrassed my mother by what'd popped from my mouth...well, I'd be even richer than I already was. "I don't know what's come over him. We have this problem at school, too. We can't always say what we want to say whenever we think it. Isn't that right, Grady? Please apologize."

"Not necessary," I assured her, grinning more widely. Yeah, I definitely liked the kid, especially when I knew now that I could probably get whatever information I needed out of the loose-lipped terrorist. "That's the thing about kids and drunks—they're always honest." I winked at Grady, then gestured for him to follow me into the kitchen. "But to answer your question, I kick ass when I'm cooking. The bigger question, little man, is what are *you* going to do to make yourself useful?"

My brow arched with mock sternness, but he wasn't intimidated in the least, which I found another point in his favor.

"I can do whatever you can do," he boasted without a hint of bashfulness but added when Lauren laughed a little nervously, "Except work the oven. Mama says I'm too young, even though I watched a YouTube video on how to work the burners and that worked out pretty good."

"What did the world do before YouTube?" I asked, only half joking because I was fairly certain YouTube was going to make college courses obsolete at some point. "But your mom is probably right about the oven. Best leave that to the adults or at least someone tall enough to ride the big-kid rides at Disneyland."

"Grady, I'm sure Nico is kidding about having you help."

"I'm absolutely not kidding. You're going to work, too," I told her, earning a wary smile. "The best way to get to know someone is in the kitchen."

"Then you're gonna find out real fast that my mom

doesn't make very good food," Grady confided, then cast his mother an apologetic look. "But you try real hard, and that's what counts."

I laughed. "Can I rent this kid for parties? He's a riot."

Lauren blushed and rubbed her hands together as she surveyed the layout of ingredients I had spread around. "Yeah, I wish I could say he was lying, but he's right. I'm all thumbs in the kitchen."

I smiled, noting that she'd changed into something far less reminiscent of a flour sack—jeans and a simple T-shirt—and unlike the ugly dress, the jeans molded perfectly to her hips and ass, blasting away the impression that she'd been hiding a less-than-stellar figure.

Hell, if I was being honest, Lauren had the kind of banging curves that always managed to turn my head. I was a sucker for wide hips, a fat ass and a small waist—and Lauren had it all. I took a brief second to whisper for her ears only, "How did you manage to hide that beautiful ass beneath that ugly dress? The jeans are a big improvement." Before she could gasp, I pulled away and continued in a normal tone, "Lucky for you, most of the dinner is already prepared and your parts are easy."

"Mama, maybe Nico can teach you a few things, too?"

Oh, little man, I'd love to teach your mama a thing or two. The thought raced across my mind, but I kept the comment behind my teeth, choosing to indulge the kid with a smile. "Sure, if your mama is open to learning, that is…"

Lauren caught the double entendre but instead of shooting me down with a look, she blushed a little, which only made me wish I could sample those pouty lips and grip a handful of that amazing ass.

Forget everything I'd said earlier about Lauren not being my type. Clearly, I was being fed bad intel because honest and true, if she'd walked in wearing what she was wearing right now, I would've changed my tactics immediately and the day would've ended with her in my bed.

Now I had to go a different route to get what I wanted.

But an easy victory was a boring one.

I pulled a chair over for Grady to stand on so he was level with the counter. "All right, little chef, you're on butter duty. I've made a garlic spread already, and it's your job to cover this freshly baked French bread with the spread so I can put it in the oven to cook. Can you handle it? I mean, it's an important job, so don't blow smoke up my behind if you're not up to the task."

Grady giggled and rolled his eyes as if I were an idiot and accepted the duty by grabbing the spreading spatula. I received an assured "I got this," and he went to work carefully spreading the garlic butter. I turned to Lauren with a cocked brow. "Now, as for you…can you manage chopping up the veggies for the salad without losing a finger?"

Lauren answered around a smile that stubbornly wouldn't stop forming. "Yes, I can handle the salad prep. I'm not a complete idiot in the kitchen."

"I don't know, junior here didn't exactly give you a glowing recommendation, and he knows you best," I said, winking at my pint-size partner in crime. The happy grin I earned twisted something unfamiliar for a brief moment, but I recovered in a blink to tease, "I'm no vampire, I don't want blood on the arugula."

Lauren laughed and shook her head, grabbing the cutting board and the assorted vegetables. "Just do your thing and I'll do mine."

"Excellent," I said, throwing some fresh basil in the sauce I'd already started the moment Lauren had left earlier that day. "The upside to being two generations removed from my Italy roots is that I was raised on solid, authentic Italian cooking and I know the difference between good parmigiana and crap."

"Do you mind if I set the recorder so we can do the interview at the same time?" Lauren asked, already reaching for her device. I shrugged as if I didn't care, but I didn't want her so focused on the interview that she completely missed all the subtle cues I was sending her way.

"Mama is a good writer. What do you do?" Grady asked. "Mama said you're just rich, but don't you have to do something to get rich?"

"Starting with the hardball questions, all right, all right," I said with an appreciative whistle. "Okay, so yeah, your mama is right, my family is wealthy, and because of that, I have a trust fund that enables me to pretty much do whatever I want—such as learn how to perfect the ultimate spaghetti dinner to impress difficult reporters."

Lauren blushed and bit her lip, no doubt to keep from skewering me in front of her kid, but I liked the way things were going thus far. In fact, the only thing that would improve the night was a glass of wine, a detail I planned to handle right now.

"My mama is hard to impress," Grady warned, finishing his butter duty. "Uncle Ronnie says it's 'cuz she's been too long without a man, but I think he's wrong 'cuz Mama has me and I'm the man of the house. I can take care of Mama just fine."

At that, I burst out laughing as Lauren's cheeks burned a brilliant shade of magenta. She fairly choked on the words, "Grady, let's go wash your hands. You're all buttery, sweetheart," before shooting me a pointed look when I struggled to contain my laughter.

"First door on your right," I managed, gesturing to the hallway, still smiling at the intel dropped from precious little Grady's gob. *So, Mama Hughes is on a bit of a dry spell, huh?* It didn't surprise me that Lauren wasn't a casual dater, especially with a kid like Grady on her heels. He probably kept her on her toes and served as an efficient cock-blocker.

I poured two glasses of 2009 Chateau Lafite Rothschild, a complex Bordeaux of red blends from Pauillac, Bordeaux, France, but I was at a loss as to what to serve Grady. I wasn't exactly equipped with juice boxes for the preschool set.

When Lauren and Grady returned, I handed Lauren her glass above her mild protests, and turned to Grady. "Here's the deal. I have water, cranberry juice and root beer. What's your poison?"

"Cranberry, please."

Odd choice for a kid but I'd oblige. "One cranberry, coming up."

Lauren explained, "Grady has a weakened kidney. It's nothing serious, but the doctor put him on cranberry juice since he was about three years old, so he developed a taste for it."

Kidney issue? I slid the short glass over to Grady. "So, it's nothing serious? What happened?"

"Mama." Grady looked at Lauren, and I understood that whatever ailed the kid embarrassed him so I dropped it.

"I'm starved," I announced, moving to the bubbling pot of pasta. I removed the pot and drained and dropped the pasta into the awaiting sauce so it could absorb some of the sauce's flavor. "In Italy, this is called *pasta saltata in padella*," I explained when I caught both Grady and Lauren watching with interest.

"Well, it smells good," Lauren admitted. "Did you learn how to make pasta from your mother?"

"Actually, a combination of my mother and the family cook, Greta. My brothers were always expected to trail after our father because of the family business, but that left me to do as I pleased. I happened to enjoy eating good food, so I naturally ended up learning how to cook for myself."

"Which no doubt has made you plenty of points with the ladies," Lauren said drily, and I didn't deny it. "Should I put that in the article, that you'll cook if she cleans?"

"Sounds like an equitable arrangement," I said, though in my head I answered a bit differently. I cook, she sucks my cock and I leave the cleanup for the maid in the morning. Not to be left out, my shaft hardened as if it were part of the main course.

Turning quickly, I took a minute on the pretense of checking the pasta, but I simply didn't want to face Lauren with a giant, inappropriate boner with her kid sitting right there.

C'mon, think of basketball, the World Series, ugh, Brussels sprouts, anything...

It was probably only seconds but it felt like a lifetime before I could reasonably present myself without sending Lauren packing with her kid under her arm to escape the rich pervert who seemed to be turned on by a terrific bowl of pasta.

Of course, that wasn't the reason, but I doubted she'd appreciate if I admitted I sprung a monster erection at the thought of her sucking my cock here in my kitchen.

"Who's hungry?" I asked, carrying the bowl to the table where I already had place settings set. Then I realized I needed another for Grady. Without missing a beat, I grabbed a plate, utensils and a linen napkin and handed them to Grady, instructing him to set his place. To Lauren, I said, "Mind if you grab the wine?"

"I probably shouldn't have any more wine," she said but grabbed the wine for me. "I still have work to finish tonight."

"Wine makes Mama sleepy," Grady chimed in, settling into the chair as if it were the most normal thing in the world to eat with a stranger. "And she has to tuck me in or else I can't sleep right."

"Is there anything this kid doesn't know?" I teased, serving up a plate for Lauren while she dished her son. "I mean, the intel I could get...it's hard not to wonder."

She graced me with a short look and reminded Grady to put his napkin in his lap before returning to her own plate with an appreciative inhale. "Well, it certainly smells incredible. Let's see if you overhyped your skills or you were uncharacteristically humble."

"Proceed. I await your opinion." I laughed and waited for her first bite.

She took an exploratory bite and closed her eyes with involuntary pleasure. "Oh, God, I can't believe I'm going to say this but...you were a bit modest in your own skills. This is the best thing I've ever had in my mouth."

SPROING!

Thank God I was seated with a napkin covering my lap. The thought of Lauren's mouth...it was too much to handle. I covered my discomfort with a wide grin. "Is that so?" I turned to Grady. "Okay, little man... what do you say? Is your mom pulling my leg or does my spaghetti truly knock your socks off?"

Grady held up his finger in a "just a minute" motion, then twirled his fork for a mouthful. After an exploratory bite, his eyes brightened and he nodded vigorously. *"Deeeee-licious!"*

Was it weird that Grady's praise made me squirm a little with pride?

I didn't know this kid. I barely knew his mother.

But everything I knew so far, I was kinda into.

A little voice warned that I was messing with things that were out of my depth.

But that was part of the allure.

Hell, I never said I was a saint and I never pretended to be. I looked to Lauren with a smile, wineglass in hand.

"Shall we start the interview?"

CHAPTER SEVEN

Lauren

As MUCH AS I wanted to find fault with Nico's culinary skills, I couldn't. He made a mean dish of pasta, and that wine pairing was divine. After listening to how Nico prepared his sauce, simmering it for hours after I left, I was embarrassed to admit that spaghetti in my house came from a jar.

"You're very proud of your heritage," I said after Nico shared some of his family's history. "How did your family go from a wine-making operation to the global empire that Donato Inc. is today?"

"Is that part of the article?" he asked, smiling above the rim of his glass, those dazzling eyes something of rare beauty. Or maybe that was the wine talking. No, I could admit he had gorgeous eyes without wanting to sleep with him. He refilled both our glasses, and even though I knew I shouldn't, I didn't stop him. Grady, having finished and becoming bored with grown-up talk, had gleefully taken up Nico's offer to level up his gamer tag on his gaming system. It would've been mean to refuse Nico's offer, but I wished I still had Grady for a buffer. "To be honest, the business side of my family's operation has never interested me. I was never in line for a serious position—my father has his heir and a spare, which makes me the spare 'spare'—so I don't really care how our family rose to the place where we are now. I reap the benefit, and that's all that matters."

"You don't mind that your father doesn't think of you in the same way as your brothers?"

"If you're asking if I have daddy issues, the answer is emphatically no. Why would I want the stress of running the empire on my shoulders? I'd much rather spend my time pursuing happy things. If you met my brothers, you'd see what I mean. It's a blessing, in my opinion, that I'm not on my father's radar."

"But that just seems wrong. A father is supposed to love his children equally." I didn't want to feel bad for Nico, but a part of me did. "I mean, what kind of relationship do you have with your father?"

Nico chuckled but I sensed I'd hit a chord. He shifted as he explained, "My father is an old-world misogynist with whom I have nothing in common, so it's safe to say I don't have much of a relationship with the old fart and I'm not missing out on anything."

"That's sad. You missed out on what it's like to have a great father. Mine died when I was fifteen, but he was my world and we were very close. Losing him still hurts to this day."

"Well, I guess I can't miss what I never had."

A true statement, but Nico's flippant shrug was incongruent with the sudden shuttering of his gaze to focus on the wine left in his glass. "Are you close with your brothers?" I asked.

"Do you have any siblings?" he countered.

"A younger sister, Claire. She's in her last year at NYU."

"And are you close?"

"Yeah, I like to think so, but the age gap makes things a little difficult at times. I mean, she's still in that college frame of mind, and I've moved on from that stage."

"Because you have a kid."

"Not only because of that but I suppose it was a big motivating factor in my need to grow up."

"So...single mom...there's a story there..." he fished, but I wasn't about to share that particular story, so I shut him down.

I placed my empty wineglass on the table and turned off my recorder. "I should probably get going. It's getting late."

Nico made a show of checking his watch and disagreed. "It's barely ten o'clock. The clubs are just starting to open. This is when the night begins."

"Not when you have a sleepy six-year-old," I said, rising. "I've already stayed way longer than I'd planned." That was an embarrassing understatement. I wasn't even sure if I had enough information for my article in spite of spending hours in Nico's company. "But I didn't count on you being a master chef and surprisingly consummate host," I admitted sheepishly.

Nico laughed, amused by my admission. A dimple in his right cheek flashed, and I felt my knees tremble suspiciously. It'd been a long time since I'd felt anything remotely resembling attraction, since Houston made his grand exit, and I didn't particularly appreciate the familiar tingle now.

Yes, definitely time to go.

I walked into the living room to gather Grady and found him sacked out. Mom guilt set in hard. I bit my lip, chagrined. "Damn it," I murmured, "he's already asleep."

"It's the pasta. Best sleeping aid in the world," Nico boasted, nodding as if he'd accomplished some great feat as to put a six-year-old to sleep.

"I hate to burst your bubble, but Grady's internal clock put him to sleep, not your pasta. My son has never had a problem dropping off, no matter where he is. I should've known better and left earlier."

"It's not the end of the world," Nico said. "Just stay."

I balked. "Excuse me?"

"Calm down, Mama Bear. I have a spare bedroom. The sheets are clean and the pillows like clouds. I don't mind if you and Grady take the spare."

"Yes, but I mind," I told him, unable to believe he would think I would stay the night with him, separate bedroom or not. The fact that my mind went some-where it shouldn't sharpened my tone. "It's not appropriate."

But he didn't seem to notice and chided playfully, "I don't get many opportunities to play the gentleman. You would rob me of the chance to play the hero?"

My cheeks flushed as butterflies erupted in my stomach. Maybe it was the wine, but he just got ten times hotter—which really should've been a crime.

"It's just not… I mean, what would people say? I have a reputation to protect. Not to mention if my editor found out…it would be all bad."

Nico still didn't see the problem. "We're adults. We're allowed to make our own choices."

"Clearly," I said with a hint of exasperation. "Which is why we both should know better."

"It's not as if I'm asking you to share *my* bed," he said, sending an illicit shiver down my backside. "Now, *that* might be construed as…inappropriate."

"Y-yes, completely inappropriate," I agreed, bobbing my head vigorously, though my stomach muscles had just tightened at the idea. "I wouldn't even consider it." What a total lie. *I'd just considered it.* Maybe for a microsecond, but it still counted.

"Neither would I."

And yet, his gaze was saying something else entirely. His gaze, if my senses weren't malfunctioning, was saying, if given half the chance, he'd fuck me raw.

My stomach tightened again. I didn't like this feeling. Everything was tingling and aware—including my lady parts, which I would've much preferred to remain silent and dead when around Nico Donato. Except, as fantasy material went…Nico was pretty hot. I wasn't above using him for mental purposes later…but to be honest, I was tired of getting myself off by myself. Just for the sake of argument, Nico might be the perfect way to scratch that itch without fear of anything turning serious, which I didn't need or want.

In that case, it wouldn't be *me* becoming a notch on *his* bedpost, but rather, the other way around. The idea had merit. Or I'd had too much wine. It could go either way.

However, for tonight, home was where I'd sleep.

"Your offer is very generous but I can't," I said firmly. "There's no way I could explain to Grady why we spent the night at a stranger's house without uncomfortable questions. You might've already noticed, he's very smart."

"A point in his favor," Nico said. "Most kids are irritating. Yours is surprisingly entertaining."

I chuckled ruefully. "Well, he has his moments, but you can imagine what kind of questions his head might conjure if we stayed."

"Fair enough but you will let me call for a car."

"I can call an Uber," I protested, but Nico wouldn't budge. There was something oddly protective about his determination to ensure our safety that plucked at my primitive female brain. I withheld a sigh of longing, wishing for a brief moment that I didn't suffer from the knowledge that all men were pigs and had ulterior motives.

Because if I *didn't* suffer that knowledge I might even enjoy an evening tangled up with Nico, skin on skin, covered in sex sweat and moaning loud enough to cause the neighbors to complain.

I rubbed my suddenly damp palms, needing to get away from Nico. Maybe Uncle Ronnie was right—it'd been too long since I'd been with a man—because I was actually starting to fantasize about banging boots with Nico Donato, a man I held zero respect for and would never trust.

But I bet the sex would be fantastic.

Of course it would be!

Watching Nico do his thing in the kitchen had been sexy as hell. A man who had the patience to simmer a sauce all day had the wherewithal to pleasure a woman with just as much attention to detail.

God, it'd been so long since I'd had sex with another human being.

On the tail of that mournful thought, Nico returned, saying, "The car is coming. He should be here in a few minutes."

"Oh! Yes, th-thank you," I said, stumbling on my words, sounding to my own ears like an idiot. I shouldered my purse and started to reach for Grady, but Nico wasn't having it and instead hoisted my boy up like he weighed nothing. Grady, adorable in sleep, his lips pursed, simply lay against Nico's shoulder as if it were natural to do so. "You don't have to do that, I can carry him," I said, troubled by how much I liked the sight of Nico holding Grady. What the hell had Nico put in that spaghetti sauce? I was clearly losing my mind.

"Nonsense," Nico said, going to the door. "Like I'm going to send you and the boy down to the car by yourselves. The city at night is no place for a mom and her son to be alone. I'll feel better knowing you made it safely to the car."

Again with the tingling. Were my ovaries doing the polka? "That's very nice of you," I said, my tongue sticking to the roof of my mouth. Maybe I'd had too much wine. I wasn't thinking clearly. But I couldn't quite help but wonder if maybe I'd misjudged Nico earlier. He'd been nothing but an entertaining and gracious host tonight. Aside from the one comment, he'd been on his best behavior.

And I hadn't hated the fact that he'd noticed my ass.

I purposefully downplayed my looks and figure because I didn't want to deal with the complications of entanglements, but I'd forgotten how good it felt to be noticed by the opposite sex.

To see that banked hunger in a man's eyes.

To know that they were interested.

But I didn't want Nico to be interested in me.

At least, the logical part of my brain didn't want that.

The decidedly female part of my brain was cooing and purring and practically begging to thrust my ass in his face.

Had I mentioned that it'd been a long time since I'd had sex? That drought was making me pretty damn thirsty right now, and Nico was starting to look like a mountain spring of cool, fresh water.

We got to the bottom floor of the building, and true to his word, a shiny black town car idled softly, waiting for us.

"Do you have a car on retainer?" I joked as Nico gently put Grady into the vehicle and strapped him into the seat belt. He closed the door gently, standing between the car and me.

"It's a perk," he answered with a cheeky grin that sent my stomach flip-flopping. I'd grown up in the city, and having a car of any sort was a luxury most people couldn't afford, except for special occasions.

"Well...um, thank you for a surprisingly lovely evening," I said, thrusting my hand toward him for a benign handshake, but Nico just stared at me with amusement as if we both knew a handshake wasn't going to happen. Instead, he accepted my hand gently and pressed a soft kiss on the top, his lips lingering long enough to create havoc with my nerve endings. The gesture was both gentlemanlike and erotic. My breath was suspiciously breathy as I said, "Th-that wasn't necessary..."

"But I disagree," he said, his gaze finding mine.

Those eyes were killers. I could only imagine how many women had fallen to their doom in their blue depths—and gladly so. "What if I said, I want to see you again?"

"I'd say that's probably a bad idea," I answered, but my belly trembled. "It would be unprofessional."

"And why is that?"

"Because it is."

"So this is it?" he asked. I jerked a nod, shivering but not because of the cold. His subtle smile was my undoing. "Well, then, if this is to be it..." and then he moved in, slowly enough that I had plenty of time to stop him, but I didn't. I tilted my chin and his lips were on mine. Electric heat zapped between us, binding us. Curse it all, I opened my mouth a little more, inviting his tongue to dance with mine. He obliged with a sexy growl that I felt to my toes. The sidewalk seemed to slant beneath my feet, and I clung to Nico, losing all sense of reason for a blinding moment. It was all sorts of wrong, but I wasn't going to see him again and it'd been so long since I'd felt a man's touch that I might've succumbed to the advances of the FedEx driver if he'd given me clear enough signals.

At least, I clung to that justification so I didn't chew myself to pieces over indulging in this single moment with Nico.

Our breath mingled as our tongues twisted, the heat building between us enough to melt snow. My clothes scratched against my skin, an irritant. It was a blessing that Nico hadn't tried to kiss me in his apartment because I might've stayed—with him, in his bed—and it probably would've been the best sex of my life.

How did I know that? Well, because *oh, God, help*

me, he was an amazing kisser and I could only imagine what he could do when given free rein.

Orgasms for days.

Yep. That was what Nico would deliver. I knew it. My certainty was bone-deep.

Argh, don't think of bone.

Time to stop. Time to be responsible.

Goddamn morals and ethics—why couldn't I just be like the rest of the women who would gladly throw their panties at his feet for a single glance from him.

Because I wasn't.

And because of that—I broke the kiss.

Reluctantly. Oh, yes, very reluctantly, but I broke it nonetheless.

"Good night, Nico," I managed as I slid out of his grasp and ducked into the awaiting car as if the devil himself were leering at my soul.

I didn't breathe until we were far enough away that I couldn't still see his silhouette watching us leave.

Then, and only then, did I draw a shaky breath, my fingers lightly touching where Nico's lips had been, closing my eyes to savor the lingering pleasure of being touched by a skillful lover…if only for a heartbeat.

CHAPTER EIGHT

Nico

I WATCHED THE car until it was out of sight.

The night had turned out like nothing I'd planned.

Never had a night bombed so bad and yet been so wonderful at the same time.

I had a raging boner—and no one to ease the pain of my erection—and yet, I couldn't stop smiling.

So, Lauren was a single mom with a fantastic ass. Never would've called that one.

Her kid was pretty chill. I didn't usually dig kids, but Grady was entertaining and smart. Kinda reminded me of myself at that age, so of course, I thought the kid was brilliant.

Under most circumstances I avoided single moms. I didn't have the patience to deal with the drama, and truthfully, I'd never met a single mother I'd felt worth the hassle to try to figure it out.

Until Lauren.

Yeah, Grady was a great kid. The little monster was different, precocious and very protective of his mom, and yet he'd spilled valuable intel with impunity.

But the kid had definitely cock-blocked me, a fact his mother had counted on.

Lauren's crafty intelligence turned me on in a way I hadn't felt in a long time.

And that kiss.

Definitely worth exploring in the future.

Except, I knew the only reason Lauren allowed the kiss was because she felt safe in the knowledge that we wouldn't see each other again.

I chuckled as I returned to my apartment. *Naive woman.* Now that I'd had a taste, I wanted more. Who took one tiny bite of New York–style cheesecake and then pushed away the plate with a satisfied "I'm good"?

Exactly. No one.

And Lauren was my New York–style cheesecake. On the surface, plain and unadorned with flash and extraneous details, but once a bite crossed your lips, you realized, nothing else was necessary. In fact, to add more would be to take away from the robust flavor of the dessert's complexity.

Lauren was smooth and rich—decadent and forbidden.

How could I not want more?

As if punctuating the thought, my erection wouldn't subside. I flopped onto the sofa as I jerked my jeans down around my hips. I palmed my cock, groaning as I closed my eyes, envisioning Lauren's sweet lips closing over the head, her teeth grazing ever so lightly as I fed my cock down her throat.

My imagination was a poor substitute for the real deal, but I'd have to make do.

I pictured Lauren between my legs, my hands threading through her thick, dark hair as her mouth slid up and down my shaft, her slender fingers gently cupping my balls as she worked my cock.

I pumped faster, hungry for the friction. In my imagination, Lauren met my gaze while her mouth worked me. I nearly lost it at the thought. I groaned more loudly as I fucked my own hand harder. My heart rate quickened as the tingling started in my balls, rattling the cages and shaking the foundation.

"Jesus, Lauren." I moaned as my orgasm hit with a ferocity I was unprepared for. I came hard, spilling everywhere as I continued to pump against my palm, gasping as my release stole my breath and left me wheezing from the sheer force.

It was several minutes before I could think again, my heart still thundering.

I rolled to the side, grimacing at the mess I'd made. I jerked my shirt off and used it to clean up, tossing it to the floor for the maid to deal with later.

A sigh escaped my parted lips and I rose slowly from the sofa, no longer suffering an erection, but the release had been only partially satisfying.

I wanted the real deal.

What did Lauren sound like when she came? Was she loud or breathy? What did she taste like? Was she sweet or musky? I liked both but I wanted to know Lauren's essence, the unique taste of her as she came, preferably when she gushed into my mouth.

Before the kiss, Lauren might've been able to play off that she wasn't interested, but that woman had set my ass on fire with her response.

She was a powder keg of need and want—and I was just the man to give her what she craved.

But she wasn't going to just give in. Lauren was too stubborn for such an easy win.

No, this situation required finesse and a certain level of clever manipulation behind the scenes to make things happen.

As I noodled the situation, my wandering gaze settled on a gilded invitation I'd tossed to the coffee table. I was expected to make an appearance, smile, nod and wave, to represent Donato Inc. Seeing as I wasn't actually needed on the business front, my brothers often threw me the public appearances.

But I needed a date.

Usually, I selected one of my regular fuck buddies, someone who understood I wasn't interested in dating, just a hot body on my arm, and an even hotter time in bed afterward. No expectations, no entanglements: a good time for everyone involved.

I wanted Lauren to be my plus-one.

Of course, she'd decline—spouting something to the effect that being my date would be inappropriate—but what if I made it impossible for her to turn me down?

A cunning smile curved my lips. All it would take would be a little nudge here, a little encouragement there and I could get Patrice, Lauren's editor, to make it happen.

But I couldn't make it look obvious or else Lauren would sniff out my hand.

Subtlety was the key.

Times were hard in publishing these days. The right dollar amount in the advertising department might grease the wheels well enough. *Luxe* could always use a high-rolling client within their pages.

Donato Inc. owned several boutique wineries—
my father collected wineries like some might collect
stamps—and it just so happened that one of the wineries was debuting a new tasting room in Manhattan.
I could run a series of ads for the tasting room, which
would be a legitimate but quite pricey expense on the
guise of promoting our little boutique winery.

The acquisition of a high-end client would tickle
the advertising execs, and Patrice would bend to whatever I asked.

Including strong-arming her reluctant reporter to
be my date for the event.

Yes, the more I gave it thought, the more the idea
had merit.

I would place the appropriate calls tomorrow.

Inordinately pleased with myself, I retired to my
bed to dream of all the dirty, delicious and downright
damnable things I wanted to do to the delectable Miss
Hughes, the hottest MILF I'd ever met.

CHAPTER NINE

Lauren

WHAT?" I ASKED, not quite sure I'd heard Patrice correctly. "I'm going where?"

But Patrice was already anticipating my refusal and frowned in my direction over the horn-rimmed glasses she insisted were the height of fashion but in my opinion only made her look like an owl.

"I don't know why you insist on being so damn difficult. It's not often that the hottest bachelor in town is willing to have you as his date at a very high-end, high-profile event."

My head was spinning. Nico wanted me to go where? "Don't you think that's a little unprofessional? The article hasn't even run yet. I shouldn't be seen out and about chumming it up with the man we're trying to tell the world is available."

"I didn't say to *date* him," Patrice said as if I were being deliberately ignorant. "And on the contrary, being seen out and about with Donato is excellent publicity for *Luxe*. You can subtly drop some hints about the upcoming feature, create some buzz."

"Did Nico put you up to this?" I asked flatly. Patrice answered with an unamused stare. I shifted, defending myself. "It just seems odd that he would pick me to go as his date. I barely know him. Surely he has other women he could invite."

"Nico has nothing to do with this. I put this in motion, not Nico," she said sharply. "I caught wind of the event, found out that Nico would be there and asked Nico if he wouldn't mind squiring you about for the sake of the upcoming article. He was a perfect gentleman about it, and I appreciated his willingness to be a good sport."

In spite of Patrice's answer, I smelled a rat. I couldn't exactly tell Patrice about the red-hot kiss Nico and I had shared a few days ago at his apartment without looking like a complete hypocrite, but there was no way in hell Patrice just casually discovered that Nico needed a date for the event.

No, this had Nico's hands all over it.

I made a show of checking my calendar. "As much as I would love to go and talk up *Luxe*, I'm busy that night."

"Busy how?" Patrice asked, her brow climbing with disbelief.

I tried not to take offense, but Patrice's constant disdain for my social life—however dull it was—got old. "I have a date," I lied.

"Yes, I know…with Nico Donato," Patrice replied, daring me to say otherwise.

"No, I mean, an actual date with a man. I mean, of course it's a man, but someone I might actually have a connection with. We've been talking for a few weeks and we've finally found time in our busy schedules to meet up. He's an engineer," I finished with a smile, seeming enamored with my fake date. I tacked on brightly, "Oh! And we have reservations at Tochi's, and you know how hard it is to get a reservation at that place. I couldn't possibly cancel on such late notice."

Patrice's mouth pursed with displeasure. "This looks very bad for *Luxe*."

I wanted to quip, *I didn't realize* Luxe *had entered the escort business*, but wisely didn't. Instead, I suggested, "Send Daphne. She'd love to spend an evening with Mr. Donato, and I'm sure it would be good for her to network for new story leads. Those dinners are terribly boring unless you know who to talk to. Daphne could use the practice."

"If I wanted Daphne, I would've given her the assignment."

I was on dangerous ground with Patrice, but she couldn't actually make me go as Nico's date, could she? I mean, surely that was breaking a few HR rules.

I held my breath as I awaited her decision. Just when I thought I was going to lose and she was going to force me to cancel my fake date, she relented with a sour look. "Well, I guess all I can say is enjoy your date. I'm sure Daphne will have a lovely time," she said, dismissing me.

Phew. Dodged a bullet. I didn't trust myself around Nico after that kiss. It was too good and I was still thinking about it way too much. That damn kiss had ignited some questionable ideas that were getting harder to dismiss—I didn't need anything to pitch fuel on the fire.

However, if I were being honest, it pinched a little at the thought of Daphne landing in Nico's arms, and that was precisely why it was the right decision to avoid him.

The man could probably convince a nun to toss her habit with one flick of that tongue, but I wasn't about to lose my fucking mind over one kiss.

But would it be so terrible to have some fun? I used to know how to have a good time, but I seemed to have forgotten the basics.

Kissing was fun; sex was better.

Just playing devil's advocate for a second…how bad would it be to have a little fun with Nico—assuming neither of us was looking for anything real or permanent?

Unlike my sister, Claire, I didn't believe in soul mates and happily-ever-after.

You know what I believed in? Hot tea with honey on cold mornings, freedom of the press and the satisfaction found in paying my own bills.

The rest was hogwash.

Maybe at one time I believed in that happily-ever-after stuff, but life had disabused me of that silliness.

I found satisfaction and fulfillment in a job well done. And as I put the finishing touches on my article on Donato, I knew I'd hit the mark. As I'd told Nico, no matter my personal feelings, I could deliver a well-written article on any subject.

I paused to admire my work, pleased with myself. Maybe Nico wasn't quite the narcissistic man-child with Peter Pan syndrome I'd initially thought, but like I'd said to Grady, Nico didn't actually do anything to earn his millions; he was a trust-fund baby, and I had a hard time respecting someone who did nothing to support themselves.

My dad had been a hard worker, and I expected nothing less from other men.

So how'd I fall in love with Houston, another trust-fund kid? Chalk it up to being young and dumb, I supposed.

Not anymore. I took pride in my ability to weed out the undesirable disguised as handsome, worldly men.

I exhaled a little too heavily even as I was mentally patting myself on the back.

Made for lonely nights, that was for sure.

The city was filled with undesirables, as evidenced by my empty social calendar.

Out of my peripheral, Daphne made her way over to me, her eyes sparkling and practically bubbling with excitement. "You are never going to believe who I'm going to accompany to the Griffin Center dinner." Daphne didn't wait for an answer before she gushed, "Nico Donato!"

I smiled, trying for some mentorly advice. "Remember, this is a business function, so don't let him put the moves on you. You're representing *Luxe*. Take this opportunity to glean some fresh story leads. If you listen carefully enough once the champagne starts flowing, you'll be surprised how easy it is to pick up leads."

But Daphne wasn't interested in career advice. "Okay, what do you think his favorite color is? I mean, black is always classy but a little funeral-ish, you know? How about a lemony yellow? I could totally rock a yellow dress, right?"

"Are you listening to me? This is not a date, and you'd do well to remember that fact. Nico is not going to fall head over heels in love with you. Likely, he'll be super charming, throw around some useless facts about the wine and then try to kiss you. Just remember...you are one of many."

Daphne made a sour face. "You are such a wet blanket. Haven't you ever just wanted to have a good time? You are the oldest young person I've ever met."

I balked. "I have plenty of fun. Loads of it, actually. I mean, crazy, wild fun, even. I just know when to do it appropriately." *Gahh, I sound like an old lady.*

"That right there means you don't have the slightest idea how to have fun."

I forced a laugh, but her comment was starting to poke at a nerve I'd never realized was tender. Was that how the office viewed me? The fuddy-duddy? Embarrassment caused me to blurt, "I'll have you know, I have a date the night of the event."

Oh, good grief, why was I pushing that ridiculous lie?

"You have a date? Like an actual date?" Daphne asked, incredulous.

The fact that Daphne found my claim hard to believe was telling. Yep, I was the office matron. "Yes, and we're going to Tochi's for dinner." I was going to hell for lying so blatantly, but I was already committed. If I wasn't careful I'd end up scrounging in the restaurant's back alley in the hopes of finding a tossed receipt that I could claim as my own for proof I'd been there. "I'm super excited. He's an engineer."

"What's his name?"

I faltered. "Um, George."

"George what?"

"George the engineer."

"What's his last name?" Daphne asked stubbornly.

"That's personal."

"I think you're bluffing."

I forced a laugh. "And why would I do that?"

"I don't know, but I'm pretty good at sniffing out bullshit, and something stinks."

"Well, I have no reason to lie." *My ego disagrees.* "Anyway, have fun, and please remember, you're representing *Luxe*." I paused, then suggested with only a dash of petty cattiness, "Wear the yellow," because unlike Daphne's inflated opinion of herself, she absolutely could not pull off a lemon yellow dress; it would make her look like a washed-out heroin addict.

And I was glad.

"Thanks," Daphne said happily, forgetting about her bullshit meter. "Have fun on your date."

The smile I'd held for Daphne's benefit dropped like a ton of bricks as soon as she was gone.

Daphne was a pretty girl. Nico liked pretty girls.

And I didn't care in the least.

Right?

Absolutely. In fact, I was totally looking forward to spending the evening cuddled up with my son, eating popcorn and watching *Transformers* (for the hundredth time). Maybe I'd splurge and order a pizza.

And maybe I'd wash it all down with a bottle of wine.

Yep, I sighed. Sounded like a solid plan.

A familiar—but solid—plan.

CHAPTER TEN

Nico

PATRICE WAS BLATHERING.

"Daphne is a great girl. I think you'll really enjoy her company. She's young and vibrant and so excited to spend an evening with you as your guest at the Griffin dinner event. Such an honor, really. Have I mentioned how excited we are at *Luxe* to feature you in our double issue? It's such a coup."

Who the hell was Daphne? No, strike that, I didn't give two shits about Daphne because she wasn't Lauren. I'd come down to the *Luxe* offices to confirm all the details, and this wasn't what I'd had in mind. I cut through Patrice's bullshit, kiss-ass routine like a hot knife through butter. "I thought we'd discussed you were sending Miss Hughes," I reminded Patrice with a subtle frown. "I have an excellent rapport with Lauren, and I was looking forward to spending the evening with *her*."

"Yes, well, unfortunately, she had a date already scheduled, and believe you me, if you knew how much that girl needs to loosen up, you'd understand why I couldn't make her cancel."

I looked at Patrice sharply. "She had a date?"

"Yes, some engineer. Said they got reservations at Tochi's. Lucky girl, right? I've heard the reservations are a bear to obtain for anyone who isn't royalty or a Donato," she said with a patronizing wink.

I didn't like the idea of Lauren dating anyone, and the fact that I didn't like it gave me pause. Should I care if Lauren was dating? She was nothing to me except an intriguing side note. Except, it bothered me. *A lot.* "Well, good for her," I murmured, seemingly in support but inside I was ordering a hit on the mystery man who wasn't me. "Although, to be honest, Tochi's is a little overrated for my tastes. To each his own, I suppose. The chef is an insufferable prick."

My thoughts churned even as I kept my expression neutral. Who was this asshole wooing Lauren? And what made him better than me? She was more than willing to turn me down—me, a Donato—and yet, she'd cut out to eat some mediocre Japanese food with some stranger?

I needed to know more about this engineer.

"Did she happen to mention a name?"

Patrice stared at me blankly. "A name? Who?"

"The name of Lauren's *engineer*," I answered, my patience thinning. "Surely, she must've mentioned a name."

Patrice appeared confused by my interest. "Not really. Lauren and I aren't exactly close. She's an excellent reporter but a bit of a cold fish. Why?"

Lauren was anything but cold. I knew that firsthand. One just needed to know how to turn up the heat. And now I was irritated as fuck.

"I hate to be a stickler for details, but our understanding was that *Lauren* would accompany me to the event and *Luxe* would reap the benefit of a new advertising client with deep pockets. By my estimation, you haven't held up your end of the bargain."

Patrice tittered nervously. "I couldn't exactly *force* her to attend the event with you without violating laws. This isn't medieval London. Surely, you can understand that. I did the best that I could."

But I wasn't feeling generous. "Obviously, your best wasn't good enough."

An uncomfortable moment passed between us. Patrice realized I wasn't kidding and paled, defending herself. "Mr. Donato, I *assure* you, I did my utmost to accommodate you in your request, but going beyond that would open *Luxe* up to a lawsuit."

I didn't care. I was too miffed about Lauren going out on a date with someone other than myself. But I supposed Patrice had a small point. I forced a smile. "Of course. I'm not accustomed to having people fail me. Forgive my manners. However, as much as it saddens me, I have to rescind my offer of patronage. If I were to forgive this incident, I believe it would set a precedent, which I feel would directly affect my family's interests. Good day, Ms. Winneham."

I started for the door, but Patrice was on my heel. "Forgive me, Mr. Donato, I had no idea how strongly you felt about Lauren. Give me another opportunity to rectify the situation."

"And how do you propose to do that?" I asked, mildly curious. "You've already claimed that you couldn't possibly put *Luxe* in a dangerous legal position, which I can understand, but I don't see what else can be done to repair our business relationship."

But Patrice had painted herself in a corner. There was little she could do to salvage my business. "We could feature you again," she suggested lamely, twisting her hands in desperation. Was I a bastard for putting the squeeze on the woman? Perhaps, but I'd already pictured the evening Lauren and I were going to have, and now it was ruined, which didn't put me in a forgiving frame of mind.

I exhaled with boredom. "I think once is plenty."

"Lauren is a very talented writer…maybe she could… write your memoirs!"

"I didn't realize *Luxe* was in the ghostwriting business," I said with derision.

"We're not," Patrice hastened to add, "but as a freelancer in a noncompeting venture…I'm sure *Luxe* would have no objections."

I opened my mouth to shoot holes into Patrice's offer but stopped short. Doing an autobiography would require hours of time spent together as she learned all about my life. I had zero interest in publishing a book, but if it meant having Lauren around on the pretense of doing the job, I was willing to play the part. But I knew Lauren would likely turn down the offer on principle alone, no matter how much I offered to pay for her services. "Your idea has merit," I admitted, though I would need to make some tweaks. The only way Lauren would take the job was if she were desperate. As if her very livelihood depended on it.

Which meant I'd have to play a little dirty.

Dirtier than usual.

"I want you to fire Lauren."

Patrice gasped, her eyes widening. "Excuse me?"

"Fire her."

"I can't do that!"

"Sure you can. Aren't you the executive editor? Or is there someone else I should speak with?"

"She's done nothing wrong, and she has a child, for Christ's sake."

I smiled. "That's not your problem, is it?"

Patrice's lip trembled as she pleaded, "Mr. Donato... please, let's talk about this."

"There's nothing to talk about. I want her fired."

"I can't fire her without cause."

"Of course you can. New York is an at-will state. You can fire her for wearing purple or chewing her food strangely. Honestly, you don't need a reason as long as the action isn't discriminatory. Blame it on budget cuts," I suggested, gesturing with a flippant motion. "But I want her done with *Luxe* by this afternoon. Are we clear?" I rose, straightening my cuffs with a bright smile to add, "Oh, and if you mention this conversation to anyone, I'll ruin you. Is that understood?"

Patrice blinked back tears but nodded. "Why are you doing this?"

I laughed. "Because I think I like her," I answered, already moving on to plan B. "Oh, and please let Daphne down gently. I won't be needing her services."

I left Patrice's office, pleased with the sudden reversal of fortune. Sometimes you had to find the silver lining.

Patrice would fire Lauren and I would hire her, turning into her knight in shining armor when she needed one the most.

Take that, Mr. Engineer. I win.

CHAPTER ELEVEN

Lauren

"I'M F-FIRED?" I stammered, tears burning my eyeballs. "What do you mean? I don't understand…was there a problem with the article? I can make changes. Seriously, Patrice…what's going on?"

Patrice was distant as she answered, choosing to avoid eye contact. "It's not my call. Budget cuts. The directive came from above. I'm sorry. We can offer a small severance package and I would be happy to provide you with references, but I need you out of your desk by this afternoon."

Was I in a nightmare? My lips were dry and my throat parched. I might even need to puke. "Patrice… please. I need this job. I've been good to *Luxe*. I don't understand."

"It comes down to dollars and cents. Basic economics. You know that the world of publishing is going through hard times, and we've been asked to make cuts. Daphne makes less than you. Therefore, losing you is the better economic decision. I'm sorry."

Patrice looked as if she also wanted to vomit, but I was too devastated to feel sympathy. I gulped down the lump in my throat and focused on the financial side of the sordid business of getting canned for the greater good. "What is my severance?" I asked.

Patrice scribbled a number on a piece of paper and slid it over to me. I gasped, definitely about to throw up. "I can't even pay one month's rent with that, Patrice. This is New York, not Kansas. Come on, you know this is bullshit."

At that Patrice cut me a short look. "I advise that you move quickly. Security will be here soon to escort you from the building, and we don't want to make a scene."

This was really happening. Patrice wasn't backing down. A terrible thought came to me, and I had nothing to lose at this point so I voiced it. "Did Nico have anything to do with this?"

"Get over yourself, Lauren," she snapped. "Not everything is some kind of conspiracy theory. It's about the budget. I'm sorry."

Ashamed, I nodded and wiped at the tears leaking down my cheek. "I'll get my things."

Patrice nodded stiffly and returned to her computer, seemingly absorbed with important *Luxe* business while my world just fell apart.

I caught Daphne's stunned expression and I knew bad news traveled fast in a small office. I lifted my chin and ignored everyone as I quietly and efficiently packed my things in a small file box, my vision blurred through a sheen of tears.

What was I going to do?

The severance was a joke. What about health care? I needed to carry benefits for Grady. I couldn't take the chance that he might relapse and need to be in the hospital. The bills would bankrupt me without health insurance.

I left *Luxe* without looking back. I took the subway instead of hailing a cab because it was cheaper and I would need every dime just to make it to the end of the month.

If push came to shove, I could probably move back in with my mom, but I was loath to do that. The woman would drive me insane within a week.

But if I couldn't pay rent…

Okay, stop freaking out. You're talented, you will find another job. I just needed to brush up my résumé and start sending out the feelers. I used to freelance. Maybe I could email a few of my old clients and see if they needed any piecework.

Or maybe I could just crawl into bed, pull the covers over my head and stay there for the rest of my life.

But what about Grady? My little sunshine. My pride stung, but maybe it was time to hit Houston up for child support. Even a little bit would help. But what if he wanted joint custody in exchange for support? I know I'd sound like a bitch if I just said, "No, I don't want you to have anything to do with my son, but if you could cut a check once a month and stay the hell away, that would be great." But damn, I wish I had that option.

I really didn't want Houston around Grady, for any reason. I didn't want Grady to turn out anything like his father, and I felt sick thinking of Houston's influence on my son. Maybe people could change, but Houston obviously hadn't changed enough to reach out in all these years.

Nico popped into mind, but I rejected anything associated with Donato as quickly as it formed.

I would save myself. I didn't need anyone else to come along and play the hero.

It was easy enough to say the words, hard as hell to stop the fear from curdling my guts.

The clock was ticking against me. I didn't have the luxury of picking and choosing; I needed a replacement job now.

New York landlords weren't known for their sympathy. If I couldn't pay, I'd get tossed out. Kid or not.

I was still stunned by the events of the day. This morning I had a job; by afternoon, I didn't.

And Patrice had never once mentioned that budget cuts may be imminent. I mean, I know the executive editor wasn't going to discuss company financials, but no matter how hard the execs tried to keep a lid on those things, inevitably, information leaked.

But nothing, not a peep had trickled down. It was as if Patrice had just woken up that morning and decided to ruin my life because I chose not to go with Nico to that stupid dinner.

Right about now I wished I'd just girded my loins and suffered through the damn event. Maybe Patrice was right and it wouldn't have mattered, but my gut couldn't quite quit the suspicion that somehow, Nico was involved.

Maybe I was being suspicious and overly harsh, especially given that Nico had been a perfect gentleman, but there were too many pieces that simply didn't fit the puzzle.

I wiped at the sweat on my brow, my pitiful box of belongings between my feet on the subway. I caught a few knowing glances, but no one engaged or asked questions. Too many people knew the walk of shame when it came to losing their jobs.

Times were hard for everyone.

Except Donato.

Yeah, it was fucking roses for the trust-fund boy.

God, I was turning into a bitter bitch.

Better to focus on the real issue—getting a new job.

I couldn't spend energy on conspiracy theories (as Patrice called them) because I needed to rebound. *Fast.*

If push came to shove, I could waitress. I held a master's degree in journalism, but waiting tables might be where I ended up.

Money well spent. I should've gone into finance. Except I hated math, and being surrounded by numbers all day made me want to jump from a window.

So, that brought me back to waitressing. Or stripping.

Fuck me. I buried my head in my hands and ugly cried.

CHAPTER TWELVE

Nico

PATIENCE WAS A virtue I didn't have, but I managed to wait three days before putting my plan into action.

I knew Lauren was probably heading into the panic zone by now, which would make the conditions perfect for my offer. I felt a little guilty for causing that panic, but I'd be remedying it soon.

It was distressingly easy to find her address—even if I hadn't had every resource available to me, a crazed lunatic could've found her address without breaking a sweat. I walked up to the older brownstone.

The neighborhood was on the decline but at one time might've been quite adorable. The buildings were in need of repair, but lazy landlords with nothing but greed on their minds had taken a toll. I hated to see formerly grand architecture disintegrate, but there were more instances of this kind of urban decay than could be fixed by one family, even one as wealthy as mine.

I pushed the buzzer and waited.

"Hello?" Lauren sounded from the intercom. "Can I help you?"

"It's me, Nico. May I come in?"

A long pause followed before Lauren said, "I don't think that's a good idea."

I cut to the chase. "I know about your circumstances. I've come to offer you a job. Are you interested?"

"How do you know about my circumstances?" she asked, suspicion in her tone. I had to tread cautiously. Lauren was smart. I had one chance to make this work.

"Look, I'm not having this conversation on the street. If you've had better offers, then I'll go, but I thought you might be at least open to hearing me out."

There was a long enough pause that I thought perhaps she was ignoring me, but finally the buzzer sounded and the interior door popped open.

I barely kept the triumph from my expression as I entered the building.

The brownstone had been converted to a duplex, and Lauren's apartment was the downstairs unit. The place wasn't awful, but I didn't like the idea of Lauren and Grady living there alone. Evidence of poor management was everywhere. The weather stripping on the interior door was rotting, which meant during the winter, the cold air probably whistled through the open crack and it wouldn't take much to kick open the streetside door if someone were of a mind to gain entry.

Muted sounds of another family living in the upstairs unit filtered down, and I shifted against the discomfort of knowing that Lauren and Grady lived in such close quarters with strangers.

I was seized by the irrational urge to tell Lauren to pack her shit—she was moving—but I knew that idea was bound to blow up like the Fourth of July when I tired of her company.

Her door opened and my heart stuttered with uncharacteristic excitement. "Nico? What's this about?" she asked, her gaze wary. Her hair was pulled back in a loose braid that draped over her shoulder. She was wearing black yoga pants with an iconic rock T-shirt. And it was the sexiest thing I'd ever seen on a woman.

That ass… I bit back a tortured groan.

"May I come in, please?" I asked. Just then Grady popped his head around his mom's thigh and grinned broadly, prompting a smile on my part, too. "Hey there, little man. Have you been taking good care of your mama?"

"Of course. Except, we're probably gonna be 'victed soon 'cause Mama can't pay Mr. Tubbins."

Lauren's cheeks flared and she practically wilted with shame and embarrassment at her son's loose lips. She threw her hands up and walked away, gesturing for me to come in as she flopped onto the sofa with a defeated expression. My conscience pinched knowing I'd put her in this position, but once she accepted my offer, all would be well—better, in fact, because I would pay her far more than that magazine ever had.

So, in a way, I was a hero. Kinda like a secret Santa.

I closed the door and took a moment to survey her small apartment. No screens on the windows. Anyone could climb the fire escape and slip into her apartment during the hot, humid summer. The aged kitchen made my eyes bleed. The carpet, worn and mashed and probably crawling with bacteria… *Good God, this is like living in communist Russia.*

I gestured to the paperwork strewn everywhere with an arched brow. "Hurricane or art project?" I asked.

"I've been going through my portfolio, looking for

the best articles to include in my job proposals. I submit electronically but I tend to think better when I have something in my hands, so I've always had paper copies of my work. But it seems no one is hiring right now. I've sent out countless résumés and offers for spec work, but I haven't had one nibble. Patrice promised me she'd give me a good reference but...I haven't had a single callback."

"I already know you're a good writer and I don't need references. I want to hire you."

"How do you know I'm a good writer?" she asked.

"Patrice let me read the copy you wrote for the feature. Very good," I lied smoothly. "Impressive. And she was the one who recommended you for the job. Seems she felt bad about having to let you go."

Lauren's surprise was colored by a touch of confusion, but she accepted my answer, immediately curious. "What do you want to hire me to do?" Before I could answer, she turned to Grady, saying, "Why don't you go watch TV in your room while I talk with Mr. Donato? We have some adult stuff to work out."

Grady rolled his eyes. "Like I don't know what adult stuff means. You can kiss him and I won't care, Mama. Like Uncle Ronnie says—"

"Grady! I'm not kissing Mr. Donato," Lauren cut in with a nervous laugh before Grady could spill more "Uncle Ronnie" gems. "We just have business to discuss and it's going to be very boring."

Grady didn't buy it, but he had enough respect for his mother to stop arguing. He disappeared into his room, but he left the door open. The more I knew about this kid, the more I liked. I didn't even try to hide my grin. "He's pretty smart."

"Too smart sometimes," Lauren grumbled, shooting me a warning look. "What kind of job are you offering?"

Instead of answering right away, I gestured to the windows. "Does your landlord know that this is a safety hazard?"

"I rarely open them, and Grady knows to stay away when they are."

"Doesn't matter. It's a landlord's responsibility to ensure that all safety laws are being upheld on his property. The weather stripping is rotten and you have cockroaches." I'd seen one on the stairs as I passed. "My guess is that if the housing authority came to inspect this property, the list of violations would be epic."

"Did you come to criticize my home or offer me a job?" she asked with a subtle scowl.

The longer I stood in this place, the surer I was I didn't want Lauren and her son living there, but one problem at a time. "I was impressed with your professionalism," I said. "I know I didn't make it easy for you, and yet, you handled yourself well. A pet project that I've been sitting on for a while returned with a vengeance, and I knew I'd finally found the person I wanted to work with."

"What project?"

"My autobiography."

She barked a short laugh. "You haven't lived long enough to be interesting enough to warrant a book about your life."

I cut her a pointed look. "You have a funny way of putting your best foot forward for a job interview."

"Is that what this is?" she asked. "Because even if you were serious...I don't think I would take the job."

"And why is that?"

"Because in all fairness, I don't know that I'm the right person for the job. I'm a journalist, not a ghost-writer. I mean, you should go with someone with more experience. If I were a different sort of person I would take your money without thinking twice, even though I've never ghostwritten anything in my life, but I'm not that kind of person."

I wasn't going to budge. "I admire your talent and I want to hire you."

"I'm flattered but…I don't know…what if you end up hating what I write?"

"Then I'll fire you and hire someone else," I said with a shrug.

She barked a laugh. "It's that easy, huh? Just throwing money around?"

"Pretty much."

Her gaze narrowed. "Let's just say for a nanosecond that I was considering your offer…what would working for you entail and what would the compensation be?"

"I would offer a lump sum for your services."

"And those services would be…"

"Ghostwriting my autobiography."

"And that's it?"

I gave her a stern look. "I would require your full attention. It would likely entail odd hours and numerous revisions. If I'm going to do this, I want it done a particular way."

"And what is the point of this autobiography?" she asked, curious.

"So the world can know my journey."

"Does the world care?"

I laughed in spite of the insult. "I'd like to think

so, but either way, as long as you're being paid, what does it matter?"

Lauren conceded my point, but she wasn't exactly sold. God, I loved how smart she was. "I don't know, Nico. I mean, I'm not entirely sure it's a good idea if we work together."

"Why not?"

A small nervous laugh escaped as she glanced at Grady's door and said, "Well, because…you know… we kissed."

"And?" I pretended ignorance. "I've kissed many people."

Her laughter faded and she glared, lowering her voice. "Yes, I'm sure you have, which is precisely why I don't want to join your roster."

"I can separate business from pleasure."

"You didn't before."

"That was *your* business, not mine," I said quietly. "Now the shoe is on the other foot. I am hiring you for your brain, not your body."

Her cheeks flared with heat, and she crossed her arms across her chest, lifting her chin to say, "Good, because I'm more than just a body. I do have a brain. And I like to use it."

"That's what I just said."

She faltered in adorable silence. I enjoyed how I kept her out of balance. Lauren never knew what to think around me because I kept her guessing. Made the game so much more fun.

"You haven't mentioned my flat fee," Lauren said, ending the whispering and drawing the conversation back to finances. "I'd need to know if it's going to be worth my time."

I chuckled at the absurdity of her statement. "I think fifty thousand is a fair amount," I said, taking immense joy in the way her eyes widened and her jaw dropped. I pretended to think she was offended. "Was that a lowball offer? I'm prepared to go to seventy-five, but that's my ceiling."

"Seventy-five thousand dollars? Are you insane?" She gasped, paling and sputtering. "Jesus, Nico. That's ridiculous! I could never accept that kind of money for such a small project."

"Ah, that's where you're wrong. It won't be small. I want you fully compensated so I'll feel justified in monopolizing your time. By the end of our agreement, you might feel seventy-five was a bargain."

She swallowed, still reeling. "Are you sure? Still… seems exorbitant."

I glanced around with open disdain. "If it means you could move out of this dump, it would be worth it," I returned to Lauren. "Did the magazine pay so little that this was your only option?"

"New York is expensive," Lauren said in her defense. "And I happen to like it here."

"I hate it," a little-boy voice floated from the recesses of the bedroom. Of course, the little imp had been listening. It's what I would've done, too. Grady appeared, crossing his arms across his chest in an identical gesture of his mother's, determined to be part of this negotiation. "One time I squished a bug when I got up to pee in the middle of the night. I'm scarred for life."

"That was pretty gross," Lauren admitted. "But struggle builds character."

"I have enough character," Grady retorted and I

laughed. Grady brightened, saying, "Are you gonna be Mama's new boss? Can we go back to your place for more *sketti*? Do you know how to make lasagna?"

A kid after my own heart. "Are you kidding? Lasagna is my specialty. I'm even better at lasagna than I am at spaghetti."

Grady grinned, turning to Lauren with a plaintive expression. "Please say yes, Mama. I'm hungry."

"It's not fair to tag-team me," she muttered, shooting me a murderous glance that I found sexy as hell. I was close to victory; I could nearly taste the triumph. To Grady she said, "Sweetheart, while Mr. Donato's offer is certainly intriguing, I have to weigh the options."

But Grady, bless his blunt heart, seemed confused. "You said we are broke. Nico is saying he'll give you money to work for him. I don't understand…seems an easy decision to me."

"I agree, Grady." I bent to agree with the boy. "But it's ultimately up to your mom."

"M-ommmmmm," Grady whined, even stamping his foot a little. "You're being *obstenacious*."

"That's not a word," Lauren corrected him. "You're trying to say either obstinate or ostentatious, neither of which apply. Sorry, future wordsmith. Better luck next time."

"Actually I have to disagree with you," I told Lauren. "I definitely feel you're being obstinate. What good reason do you have to turn down my offer aside from your pride? Seems kinda immature when the stakes are so high."

"I have to do what's best for me and Grady," Lauren started, but I wasn't going to let her wiggle out of this one.

"And providing for yourself and your son seems a solid decision, while turning your nose up at a lucrative offer out of some misplaced pride is just shortsighted, wouldn't you agree?"

She laughed. "I see what you're doing. On the surface, you're using logic to prove your point, but you and I both know that there's more to your offer, and it's an insult to pretend otherwise."

The subtle twinkle in her eye gave her away; she was enjoying the game.

I smiled, slow and sure. "The ball is in your court. Do you want the job or not?"

A pregnant pause stretched between us as Lauren considered my offer. "Fine," she finally said, but before I could crow, she tacked on, "but there's going to be nothing but professional behavior between us, got it?"

"Of course," I agreed with a solicitous nod that reeked of total bullshit and she knew it, but this was half the fun, this subtle undercurrent of tension that coursed between us. I couldn't wait to put her in my bed. I rubbed my hands together, pleased with my victory and practically clicking my heels together. "Pack your bags. You and Grady are leaving this dump. Until we can find you more suitable housing, you and the boy can stay with me."

"Yay!" Grady jumped up and down, shaking his little butt in a makeshift boogie with such spirit, his glasses nearly bounced from his nose.

"Whoa!" Lauren rushed to put the kibosh on Grady's celebration. She looked to me as if I'd just suggested we go jump from an airplane without parachutes. "Are you insane? We can't just move in with you."

"Okay, I get it. It's unorthodox but I'm about to drop a significant investment in your services. I don't trust that this place is safe. If something happens to you, I'm out a lot of money. Think of it this way…I'm ensuring the job gets done."

"Yeah, Mama, it's just *ecobomics*," Grady added helpfully, and I wanted to high-five him.

Lauren bit back a grin at her son's attempt but said, "I don't live in the ghetto, and you're being a snob. This place is very cute, and I like it."

I tried not to roll my eyes and instead turned to Grady. "How about lasagna tonight?" Grady nodded vigorously. "Then we better find a way to convince your mama to stop wasting time and get to packing."

"I'm going with Nico!" Grady shouted, burning out of the living room to his bedroom to pack.

I smiled at Lauren. "I think working together is going to be loads of fun. Don't you?"

"I think you might be the devil." But her smile said the opposite.

"I might be," I agreed, then gestured before checking my watch. "Go pack. The car will be here shortly, and if I'm going to start the pasta, I need to get going quickly."

She shook her head, snickering. I could tell she thought I was biting off more than I could chew. Maybe I was—I'd never lived with a single mom and her kid, but I was eager to give it a shot. Seriously, I hadn't looked forward to anything this much since…hell, I couldn't even remember.

Lauren walked backward slowly, pinning me with her gaze, saying, "You're going to regret this," but I got the impression that was the part she was looking

forward to, and that turned me on like you wouldn't
believe.

I fully planned to have Lauren eating out of my
hand, sucking my cock and falling in love with me
before she even realized how it'd happened.

God, I love the game!

CHAPTER THIRTEEN

Lauren

THE HUM IN my body corresponded with the ridiculous curve of my lips that I couldn't ignore as I packed.

Was this really happening?

I grinned as I bypassed my everyday, functional underwear and deliberately grabbed my pretty, rarely worn and uncomfortable panties that I always avoided in favor of comfort.

Yep, I thought as I stuffed the panties into my suitcase, this was totally happening.

Okay, so time to get real. Nico was hot. Nico wanted to have sex with me. Forget all that bullshit he tried to feed me about this "being business." I could see in his eyes that he wanted me.

Felt good to be wanted.

The thing about single motherhood, sometimes you forgot that you were sexy at one time.

But when Nico looked at me—I remembered.

A shiver danced down my skin.

And I missed that feeling.

So yeah, I was packing my suitcase to go work for Nico. I could pretend to hold the line and say I wasn't going to sleep with him because I had more integrity than that, but let's get real, I was only human—and I missed sex.

And I'm not talking about *good* sex, I meant sex, period. At this point, I might settle for a quick grope and poke, but I knew in my gut that Nico would make a night out of whatever sexual circus he had planned in his head.

My toes curled at the thought.

The other part of this equation was the reality I didn't have time to wait out this hiring freeze. Publishing was in a total state of ever-tightening budgets, and it was going to take more time than I had to find a new job.

And fifty thousand dollars—I still couldn't quite believe that offer was real—would allow me to find a quality job rather than a hurried one.

But I would make it clear that Grady wasn't part of the negotiation. I didn't need Nico messing with his head. As far as Grady was concerned, Mama was just doing a job and that's all he needed to know—even though Grady had been suspiciously happy to toss me into Nico's lap. I would've thought Grady might be more resistant to the idea of another man coming into my life.

Go figure.

Finished, I went to Grady's room to find him sitting on his overstuffed suitcase in order to zip it.

"What did you pack?" I asked, laughing. "Let me take a look." My eyes widened as I saw the contents of every drawer and an assortment of toys jammed in the suitcase. I looked at Grady, shaking my head.

"Honey, we're not staying forever. I don't think you need all of this."

"Nico said to pack everything that mattered to me," Grady said, lifting his chin. "He also said we're not coming back to this dump."

Of course Nico said that to my impressionable son. First order of business…set Nico straight on the boundaries. However, I needed to get Grady to understand, too. "There's nothing wrong with our little apartment. We've made a lot of great memories here," I said, pulling things to prioritize spring clothing so the suitcase could close. "Think of this as a vacation. It's nice to visit someplace fun and different, but all things—even fun things—come to an end and then we return home."

Nico appeared in the doorjamb and said, "Don't worry, little man. I'll work on your mom. In the meantime, let's shake a leg. This place gives me hives."

"It would do you some good to live like a normal person," I said to Nico, thrusting Grady's luggage at him. "Make yourself useful and carry this, please."

Nico grunted at the impact but chuckled at my ire. "So sassy," he murmured, amused. He grasped Grady's hand and said, "The car is here. Let's get you loaded in while your mama finishes up her own packing."

Protests died on my lips when I saw how Grady gripped Nico's hand with total trust, as if they weren't practically strangers. How did Nico have this hold on my kid? I was baffled at how easily the man had Grady twisted around his finger. It also worried me. I wasn't going to let my son fall in love with Nico only to have Nico disappear when it no longer amused him to play house.

Sex was one thing; messing with my kid's head was another thing entirely.

A few moments later Nico returned just as I was locking the apartment. He relieved me of my luggage, his smile bright and engaging, but I stopped him with a warning. "Don't you dare break my son's heart, do you hear me?" I said, my tone low. "He's just a little boy. He won't understand when you lose interest and ditch him. Whatever this arrangement means in your head, just know that Grady is off-limits."

"You worry too much. I'd never hurt a kid."

Even if he believed that, I didn't think he understood how his actions could affect a vulnerable six-year-old. "For whatever reasons, Grady seems to like you. Don't make me regret taking this deal. If you break my son's heart, no amount of money will make his pain worth it."

"Down, Mama Bear," he said, that dimple popping as he grinned. "C'mon, the car is waiting."

The Donato name on my résumé could put me in front of the right people. He had a spacious two-bedroom apartment (it was bigger than some houses in the city) and it was, admittedly, in a nicer stretch of the city than my own apartment.

I was going to treat this unorthodox situation as a working vacation with superfancy amenities—and possibly fringe benefits.

"This is going to be fun," Nico said, handing the luggage to the driver. "I've never had roommates before."

I resisted the urge to roll my eyes. "Famous last words," I retorted as I stepped inside the car to join Grady.

Nico joined us seconds later. From the outside looking in, we appeared a family. I tried not to give the pinch that followed much thought. I'd long given up the idea that I might find someone to fill in the role of daddy and husband. I prided myself on being self-sufficient, and to this point, I had been.

But I wasn't going to lie…a part of me wished life had dealt me a different hand. I hadn't realized what a douche nozzle Houston was until it'd been too late.

I wouldn't make the same mistake twice.

And, to date, I hadn't.

But then, I hadn't actually *dated* either. The idea of allowing someone into my life for anything more than superficial gave me anxiety. Breakups were messy, and I couldn't take the chance that Grady might get hurt in the crossfire.

The easiest solution was to avoid dating.

Which meant no sex.

No companionship.

No one to snuggle with and watch corny television shows.

At this point, I feared my vagina might have cobwebs.

And to add a little more anxiety to the mix, I recently read an article that said without regular sex, a woman's vaginal walls atrophied! I might have an old-lady vag by now!

I searched but the article didn't state how quickly this process happened. Hopefully, the process hadn't already begun for me.

I snuck a quick look Nico's way, my breath catching. Damn, the man was hot. I'm talking hotter than a New York sidewalk in July. Throwing pride and what-not aside, I couldn't imagine a better candidate for the job of reintroducing me to orgasms without the aid of a vibrator than Nico Donato.

The question was…should I make the first move or wait and see what Nico put into play first?

Maybe I'd have to play it by ear.

CHAPTER FOURTEEN

Nico

I COULDN'T BELIEVE my good fortune. I truly didn't believe that Lauren would cave so easily. I thought for sure I was going to have to add a little more spice to the pot, but Lauren was a terrible negotiator and I'd gotten off easy.

Fifty thousand was chump change. I could spend that in a weekend with the right motivation.

It felt good to spend it on Lauren knowing that she needed it so desperately. I'd never played the hero before, and it was almost addictive.

Generally speaking, I steered clear of women in financial straits because, well, they became needy and clingy within a heartbeat, and that irritated the fuck out of me.

But Lauren didn't act like a desperate woman. She acted like a boss with her own agenda, and that fired me up. We were two predators circling each other, looking for the weak spot. Except she had a banging body and when I was around her, I sprang boners at the most inopportune moments.

Which only made our exchanges even more entertaining.

Ha! I know, crazy.

"Mama made me put back some of my toys," Grady
said, looking to me.

"No worries. I can replace whatever you left behind," I assured him, already planning in my head
an epic shopping spree at whatever toy store the kid
wanted.

"That's not necessary," Lauren said, shooting down
my offer. "He doesn't need any new toys. He brought
plenty. Trust me, you'll thank me the first time you
see his toys strewn about like a hurricane has come
through your apartment. Or the first time you step on
a Lego with bare feet."

"I have a maid. I doubt it'll bother me."

"You have a maid?" Grady said, impressed. "That's
so cool! Does she clean whatever you tell her to?"

"Grady," Lauren admonished, but I enjoyed the
boy's enthusiasm. Still, Lauren was quick to say, "I'm
sure Mr. Donato cleans up after himself. Just because
he has a housekeeper doesn't mean he's a slob."

Her pointed look punctuated her statement, and I
actually felt a twinge of embarrassment. I couldn't say
that I gave the housekeeper much thought beyond that
she came each day to clean up after me.

"Stop calling me Mr. Donato," I said. "I told you
it makes me feel like an old man. Besides, now that
we're going to live together—"

"This is temporary," she cut in with a firm reminder
above Grady's head for emphasis. "*Temporary.* Like a
working vacation for us."

"Of course," I conceded but added, "but until you

guys go home, I would appreciate it if you'd stop calling me Mr. Donato. Gives me diarrhea." I faked a shudder. "And makes me feel old."

"Fair enough," Lauren said, surprising me with her agreement. "While we're staying with you…we'll call you Nico."

Grady was watching us go back and forth, his eyes bright. I wondered what was going through his head, though. It also made me wonder why his father wasn't around. Lauren had deemed that information off-limits, but I wanted to solve the mystery. Why wasn't the father part of Grady's life? Was he a deadbeat dad? A criminal? I wasn't exactly of the opinion that boys needed their fathers, if those fathers were assholes. Lauren had done a pretty good job with the boy to this point, so I wasn't about to spout off something ridiculous.

Not to mention, I doubted saying something like that would make points.

And seeing as all this elaborate scheming had one goal—getting Lauren into bed—I wasn't going to waste time on things that created obstacles.

"I'd like to draw up a contract to detail my responsibilities and your expectations as well as the monetary compensation," Lauren said.

I nodded. "Of course. I can have the appropriate contract drawn up by tomorrow."

"Once we've both signed, we can start," she said with the sharp air of a proper professional. "I would also like to use this project on my résumé."

I shrugged. "Fine." But I didn't want to talk business so quickly. I wanted to get back to the part where Lauren's tongue danced with mine. I was impatient to put circumstances into play, but I had to tread carefully or everything would fall apart, leaving me with an awful case of blue balls—again. I turned to Grady. "Are you in school?"

"Yes, kindergarten," he answered proudly. "I know all my numbers and letters already and I can write my name."

"Excellent. Very important set of skills," I said, earning a small smile from Lauren. "And which school do you attend?"

"Langston Primary."

"Public school," I surmised, looking to Lauren. She answered with a nod. "Is it a good school?"

"It is," Lauren answered, casting me a warning look. I supposed I should back off. I couldn't very well agree to finance Grady's future education when I might lose interest in both of them within a month. Still, I didn't know anything about this Langston Primary, and a child as bright as Grady should have the best. But I had to shelve that thought for now because the car had arrived at my apartment.

I grabbed both suitcases from the trunk while Grady skipped ahead to the doorman. I'd already informed Jepperson that I would be having guests for the next month, so the man was appropriately friendly to the little boy.

"He's nice," Grady said. "He gave me a sucker."

Lauren gasped and relieved Grady of his candy. "You know better than to accept candy from a stranger, Grady!" she said, tossing the candy in the trash can by the elevator. "Honestly, the rules haven't changed just because we're staying somewhere fancier than our place." To me, she said, "Please let your doorman know that he's not to give my son candy."

"He was just being friendly," I said, defending Jepperson. "He's been my doorman for years. I doubt he'd do anything so stupid as to dose my guests."

"When you have kids, you'll understand."

I doubted I'd ever have children so her point was lost on me, but I agreed nonetheless. "I'll let Jepperson know."

"Thank you."

To Grady, I winked privately, earning a grin. My heart gladdened to see the scowl lift from Grady's mug. I was already getting attached to the kid, which probably wasn't a good thing, but I'd worry about the consequences later.

We entered my apartment and I was irritated to see my brother lounging on the sofa, flipping through channels as if he owned the place.

Okay, technically, the apartment was owned by the family trust, but it was still my apartment and I regretted letting him have a key.

"What are you doing here, Dante?" I asked.

But Dante was more interested in my guests, tossing the remote to stare at Lauren and Grady as they stood nearly frozen at the sight of my glowering older brother. "I didn't realize you were having a sleepover," he drawled.

"Well, you didn't ask." To Lauren, I said, "Go ahead and get settled while I talk with my brother."

Lauren hustled Grady into the spare bedroom and closed the door.

Turning to Dante, I didn't hide my irritation. "What the actual fuck are you doing here?"

"I could ask you the same thing."

"I live here."

He gestured toward the spare bedroom, where Lauren and Grady had disappeared. "I'm talking about your guests. Something smells off, even for you, little brother. Whatever you're doing, it better not look bad for the family."

"It has nothing to do with the family and it's none of your business. I'm just helping out a friend."

"A friend? Who is she?" Dante asked.

"What does it matter?"

"Because I don't trust that you're not up to something, and whenever you mess around, it always seems to find its way back home. I won't have you upsetting Mamma with your bullshit. She hasn't been feeling very well."

"What's wrong with Mamma?"

"Nothing serious but Luca's wedding took a lot out of her, and she can't seem to find her energy again."

I was closest to our mother. It bothered me that I hadn't noticed, but then Mamma had a tendency to pretend all was well, even when it wasn't. I think it was a survival method having been married to my father since she was a teen. To say my father was a difficult man was an understatement.

"I'll go see her tomorrow," I said. "Is that what you came to tell me or did you come to lounge on my sofa and eat all my food?"

"No, I was in the neighborhood and I came to confirm that you'll be representing Donato Inc. at the Griffin dinner. You haven't RSVP'd yet and the event is around the corner."

"I'm going," I said, but I didn't want Lauren hearing about the dinner before I could convince her to be my date. "Stop being such a micromanaging asshole. I said I'd go, so I'm going. You don't need to babysit me."

"Stop acting like a child and I'll stop feeling the need to babysit."

Dante always treated me like a kid. It didn't matter that I was a man. All Dante saw was the little brother.

It was annoying as fuck.

"Now, what's the story with your friend?" Dante probed, and I wanted to kick his ass out. "I've never known you to befriend women with kids."

"There's a first time for everything," I quipped, moving to the kitchen, hoping he'd get the hint and leave. "If that's all you needed…I have pasta to make."

"Pasta? What are you making?"

The door opened and Grady burst from the room with Lauren chasing after him. Clearly, he'd had enough of being cloistered, not that I blamed him. "Who are you?" Grady asked without a hint of bashfulness.

Dante drew himself up to tower over the kid, but Grady didn't budge. Lauren nervously thrust her hand toward Dante, introducing herself. "I'm Lauren Hughes. This is my son, Grady. We're guests of your brother's while I write his autobiography."

At that Dante shot me an incredulous look. "Autobiography? What fucking bullshit is this?"

"You said bad words. You're going to need to put two dollars in the swear jar," Grady said with the seriousness of an IRS agent come to perform an audit.

I barked a laugh at Dante's startled expression as I shrugged. "The kid is right. You better watch your mouth or you're going to fund Grady's college tuition."

"Sorry, kid, I'm not accustomed to my brother having anyone under eighteen in his apartment," he said. "But my question stands. Why the hell are you doing an autobiography? You haven't done anything of interest or value in your whole life, unless partying and wasting money are a skill set worth talking about."

"It works for anyone currently in reality television," I answered, my hackles rising. Just because I hadn't been groomed for the family business didn't mean that I was without any skill or talent. It was the same fucking argument with Dante, and it drove me nuts. I purposefully stuffed a preemptive five-dollar bill in a glass and said, "If you're through being an asshole, would you mind getting the hell out? I have plans, and they don't include sparring with you over bullshit family crap."

The tension in the room was uncomfortable. Lauren looked ready to pack Grady up and bail, but she didn't. Dante shot me a look that promised a conversation at a later date but grabbed his keys and headed for the door until Grady stopped him.

"You still owe the swear jar, Mister."

Dante shook his head and looked to me, saying, "Nico can cover my bill. It's about time he paid for someone else's problems instead of the other way around."

And then he slammed out of the apartment.

I met Lauren's questioning gaze, and I was embarrassed that she'd seen Dante tear me down. Lauren had inadvertently poked at a tender nerve the other night when she'd told Grady that I didn't do anything. Dante seemed to go out of his way to make sure I always knew that I was extraneous—useless.

And it never failed to hurt no matter how many times I told myself I loved not having to shoulder any responsibility for the Donato legacy.

Yep. I loved my freedom.

Dante could go fuck himself.

CHAPTER FIFTEEN

Lauren

I WANTED TO ask Nico about his brother, but I could tell from his expression he wasn't in the mood to share—and frankly, it wasn't my business. Whatever struggles created friction in Nico's family were beyond my pay grade, and I didn't want to get involved.

Even though Dante Donato was intimidating, I bristled for Nico.

But what good would come of admitting that I thought Nico's brother was a total ass? Family was still family. At times I thought my sister, Claire, was the spawn of Satan, but I'd fight anyone to the death if they said anything crappy about her. I imagined the same rules applied for Nico. So, it was best to keep quiet.

Dinner, just as before, was fantastic—eating pasta every night was going to destroy my waistline, but it was so hard to turn down good food made by someone else. And Grady, as picky as he was, gobbled up whatever Nico put in front of him. I didn't know if Grady was trying to impress Nico or if he truly just loved the man's cooking, but either way, I was discomfited. I was trying to get out of this situation without permanently damaging my kid, but so far, I wasn't sure if I was succeeding.

Except Grady seemed fine. I'd never seen him clean a plate so quickly—and ask for seconds.

But soon enough it was time to put Grady to bed. After a quick bath and story time, I tucked Grady into the bed and kissed his sweet forehead. Although he was yawning and ready to sleep, I took the opportunity to reiterate how temporary this arrangement was, just to be on the safe side. "Sweetie, I know you love Nico's cooking and Nico has a very nice apartment, but we can't stay forever. He has a life and we have our own life that we will get back to after my job is finished."

"I know, Mama," he said, cracking a yawn. "But I like Nico. He's funny and I like the way he looks at you when you're not looking. It's all warm and fuzzy-like. Kinda how Auntie Claire looks at pumpkin pie with whipped cream at Thanksgiving."

I smothered a laugh. "Auntie Claire does love her pumpkin pie, doesn't she?" Grady nodded, tucking his hand under his chin. I smoothed the hair from his eyes. "But as pumpkin-pie awesome as Nico may seem…I don't want you to get your hopes up for nothing."

"Okay, Mama," Grady said, his eyes fluttering shut. "Night. Nico says tomorrow we're going sailing and I need my rest."

Sailing? What the hell? I pressed another kiss to my son's head and closed the door behind me.

I found Nico on the sofa, a glass of wine in hand and a glass waiting for me on the coffee table. "What's this about sailing?" I asked with a frown. "Grady said you told him we were going sailing tomorrow."

"I did."

"He has school."

"What's one day of missed kindergarten?" he said, waving away my objections. "Come, sit. Try the wine. It's from a boutique winery my family owns, and it's quite good."

I bristled a little that Nico hadn't asked me first, but there was no way Grady was skipping school. I'd make that clear in the morning, but for now, I accepted the wine. "You have to be careful around Grady. I don't want him hurt."

"I understand."

He was being truthful, even if he didn't realize how easily a kid's heart could get trampled. I sipped my wine, nodding with approval. "It's good," I murmured.

Nico surprised me by asking, "You haven't dated since Grady was born?"

I bit my lip, embarrassed to admit, "No."

"And by that I assume, that means…"

My cheeks heated. "You assume correctly. I haven't had sex in six years."

"Good God, woman, that can't be healthy," Nico said, only half joking.

"According to an article I read in *Women's Health*, it's not. Apparently, vaginal atrophy is a thing I need to start worrying about, on top of everything else that sits on my shoulders."

"To be honest, if I were a woman, that would scare the hell out of me. I mean, vaginal atrophy, that sounds awful."

"Yes," I agreed, still embarrassed but somehow finding the humor, "it is awful and sad."

"Let me get this straight…you don't get laid be-cause…you think it will affect Grady somehow?"

"It sounds weird when you put it that way. What I mean is, *personally*, I don't like one-night stands, so in order to have sex, I have to have feelings for the guy, and you can't develop feelings unless you spend time together. Babysitters cost money and I'm a single mom on a budget, so that means, by way of simple process of elimination, I don't get sex."

"That's the saddest story I've ever heard."

I barked a short laugh. "Yeah? You should see my checkbook. That story will make you weep." I amended my statement with, "I mean, before I accepted your offer."

"Let me make you an entirely separate proposal, no money involved," he said, surprising me. When I frowned in confusion, he said, "Look, I truly like you. Your kid is fantastic, and I don't say that about most kids. I understand your reasons for staying away from random hookups—in this day and age, it's probably not a good idea for a single mom anyway—but at this rate you're going to be a spinster by the time you get some action, and that just kills me."

"Oh, does it?" I said wryly, sipping my wine. "Please continue."

"You're a vibrant and fucking sexy-as-hell woman. No need to mince words. I'm just throwing it out there. It's a tragedy to let the prime years of your life slip away because you're too afraid to grab on to some pleasure for yourself. You're a great mom—I can see that plain as day—but you were a woman before you became a mom, right?"

"Well, yeah," I said, shaking my head. "But I was a lot of things before I became a mom. Not everything can be reclaimed from your youth."

"Your sex life can be," he returned simply. "Hear me out…we're not trying to catch feelings, that's when things go sidewise and kids get hurt. Whether we're fucking or not…I still want to be your friend. I mean, like I said, you're a pretty cool person and I want to get to know you better. And not just in the bedroom."

I tried not to smile above the rim of my glass. *And it starts…* "Don't you think that might compromise our working relationship?" I asked. "What if we aren't compatible in the bedroom? We'd have to still work together long enough to finish the job I was hired to do."

He waved away my concern with annoyance. "Forget about the money. I'll have it wired to your account tomorrow, and whether things go sour or the job falls apart, you'll still get paid. You can rest easy on that part."

I gulped the final swallow of wine, silently amazed at how flippantly he threw hundred-dollar bills around like confetti on New Year's Eve. "You're saying you'd pay me before the work was done?"

He shrugged. "I trust you."

I released a shaky breath. "But why? You barely know me."

"I have a good sense about people."

"Yeah? And what do you sense about me?"

He gently took my empty wineglass and set it next to his before coming closer to peer into my eyes. "You really want to know what I thought when I first saw you?"

"Aside from my ugly dress," I reminded him, trying to hold on to some kind of levity to prevent any actual sincerity on his part to touch me.

Nico smiled, but his gaze was burning into mine. "I

saw a woman I knew I had no business thinking about in any sort of way."

"And why is that?" I asked, barely able to manage the words with Nico's lips so close to mine.

"Because you were a woman too good for someone like me," he admitted before closing over my mouth, stopping whatever protests may have arisen, the tease of his tongue reminding me how much I'd missed being in the arms of a man, how desperate I was for physical contact of an adult sort.

And Nico was a master with that mouth of his. I had no excuse. I knew I was playing with fire, but somehow the burn felt so good. The warmth of his masculine scent filled my senses, intoxicating me in the most addictive way.

He slowly pulled me closer and I went willingly, the press of his hands against my back a welcome pressure. I missed the confidence of a good lover, the feel of a man's hands firmly guiding me.

Nico instinctively knew when to push and when to let me lead, creating a dance that built an ever-increasing tempo.

"You're the most incredible woman I've ever met," Nico admitted, his voice a soft caress against my nerves. "I've been all around the world and never had the privilege of having someone like you in my arms."

How could I not melt? But if we were going to do this, I needed boundaries of some sort. "You have to promise to be discreet for Grady's sake," I said, breathless. "Promise?"

"Baby, I'll promise you the fucking moon, if that's what you want," Nico growled, his eyes burning with the same hunger as his arms tightened around me.

"I don't want the moon...just your promise that we'll keep this on the DL. I can't have Grady hurt."

"Deal," he said, sealing his mouth to mine with an urgency that I mirrored.

Holy fuck. This is really happening.

He led me to his bedroom. And once the door was closed, I couldn't get my clothes off fast enough.

For the record, I'm not sure who seduced whom first.

Maybe it was a draw.

CHAPTER SIXTEEN

Nico

I KNEW I should've been crowing with victory, but somehow Lauren's sudden change of heart made things ten times more real—the stakes so much higher.

My hands trembled as I unhooked her bra, my nerves drawn tighter than a virgin's on prom night.

I wanted everything to be perfect. I wanted to leave her breathless and moaning and wondering how the hell she'd ever survived without my cock inside her.

The pressure to perform was creating all sorts of havoc on my Johnson.

I sucked in a wild breath as her breasts came into view. "Perfection," I murmured, the word slipping from my mouth without thought.

Lauren blushed, vulnerable, and I knew she felt self-conscious about the faint, silvery lines caused by her pregnancy, but all I saw was beauty. My throat closed as I reached for her, pulling her close. I wanted to taste every inch of her body, to show her with my touch that I thought she was the sexiest female I'd ever laid eyes on, but my hands were shaking like an addict needing a fix and I was the one embarrassed.

"Have you changed your mind?" Lauren asked, anxious.

"God no," I answered, adding, "I'm fucking nervous as hell, though."

"You? Nervous?" Lauren repeated, confused. "Why?"

I couldn't give her a coherent answer without screwing up the moment. To admit that I was scared of underwhelming her, knowing I'd have one shot to make it right, was messing with my mojo. Instead, I scooped her into my arms, shocking her with the sudden motion. She instinctively wrapped her arms around my neck. "Less talk, more action," I said with a grin. When in doubt, let muscle memory take over.

I laid her on the bed and immediately climbed her body, her taut, dusky nipples begging for my mouth. An urgent need to know her taste, her unique flavor, egged me on, and I obliged my desire without hesitation.

She gasped as my mouth closed over her tightened bud. Lauren arched as I suckled, my hand sliding down her trembling belly to find her neatly groomed pussy. God, I wanted to bury my face between those dewed lips. I was like a kid in a candy store, eager to taste everything I could stuff in my mouth.

I slid my finger between her folds, gently probing to find her G-spot with my middle finger. I listened to her subtle cues to zero in on the exact spot that made her shake and quiver, then I slid down to that sweet pussy and dived in.

Spreading her long legs, I lost myself between her slit, seeking and destroying her swollen clit, sucking and teasing until she was gasping and biting her lip to keep from crying out. Somehow, knowing she couldn't let loose because of Grady sleeping in the other room made the entire situation hotter. I wanted her to lose control, to thrash as if a demon were being unleashed inside her. I slowed, only to start again, pushing her harder, deeper into that pleasure abyss of total meltdown. Her thighs quivered as the rapid rise and fall of her chest gave away her nearing release. I pushed her harder, needing to feel her come beneath my tongue, needing to hear those unbridled cries as she crashed.

And God, I wasn't disappointed.

Lauren came with the sweetest cry as she gushed against my mouth. I lapped at her, enjoying every drop, relieved that I could make her come that hard.

"Nico," she whispered when she could speak, her voice raspy as her head lolled on the pillow. "Holy fuck…"

I grinned, rising to seal my mouth to hers again, wanting her to taste herself on my lips. Some women shied away from their own scent but not Lauren. The beautiful heathen kissed me hard, our tongues twinning against one another like drunken snakes in a ritual dance of courtship. My cock hardened to the point of stone; any harder and the skin would've split.

I couldn't wait any longer. I made quick work of sheathing my cock in a condom and then breached her slick folds, splitting her apart with a guttural moan of pure pleasure.

Liquid heat closed around my shaft, and I lost the ability to think for a moment, so lost in the incredible sensation of being inside Lauren.

It was as if she were made for me. I'd fucked a lot

of women, but they all faded from memory as soon as I was skin to skin with her.

I was too lost to realize how worrisome that should've been.

All that mattered was this moment.

I lifted her legs onto my shoulders and drove deep, grinding against her G-spot with unerring accuracy. I wanted to hear her come again and again. I didn't think there would ever be a time when I tired of that sound. Her lovely legs, strong and sleek, were up around my ears as I bent her in half, drilling her with my entire length, fucking her so deep that my balls slapped against that plump ass. *Jesus, has sex ever been this good with anyone else?* I didn't have the mental brainpower to do more than focus on building the heat between us. I needed her release so I could claim my own, but I was already losing the battle. My ability to control the need to come was becoming shaky at best.

"L-Lauren," I choked out, my balls tightening as everything began to clench in preparation for launch. "Holy fuck...I can't stop..."

But Lauren was right there with me. Stiffening, she cried out, almost sobbing as she came again, and I groaned as I came harder than ever before, jetting over and over until I was left with absolutely nothing in my body. Everything pulsed wildly as pleasure blotted out rational thought and I floated in a pool of total bliss.

Somehow I had the wherewithal to roll away and toss the used condom into the bedside trash before collapsing beside her, my breath harsh, my heart thundering.

We remained side by side, struggling to catch our breath. I didn't want to talk. Talking would only shed light on something that I didn't want to see clearly. I wanted to curl my arms around her, drawing her against my front, and fall asleep.

Holy Jesus, I wanted to...*cuddle*?

But Lauren did us both a solid and climbed from the bed, scooping up her discarded clothing with a glee-fully whispered "Thank you, I needed that," before slipping from my bedroom, leaving me alone.

Which should've been ideal.

How many times had I wished the women I'd brought home would take themselves away so I didn't have to lie there, uncomfortable and wishing I had the entire bed to myself?

Lauren had done that. *Wham, bam, thank you, dude*, and she was gone.

I drew the blankets up around me, feeling ridiculously vulnerable. I wanted to march into the spare bedroom, scoop her up and return her to my bed.

Which, of course, would blow out of the water our agreement to keep things discreet and on the DL.

I wasn't accustomed to taking the needs and wishes of other people into account.

Couldn't say I liked it either.

For Grady's sake, I would adhere to Lauren's wishes.

Getting her into bed had been the deceptively easy part, I realized. Hiding the fact that I wanted to keep her there was going to be the hardest thing I'd ever done.

CHAPTER SEVENTEEN

Lauren

"Mama, you're humming," Grady remarked as I rummaged around the kitchen, looking for something to make for breakfast. I whirled around, a guilty smile forming as I tried to tamp it down. "I bet you had a good sleep. Nico's bed is really comfy."

"Yes, it was very nice," I agreed, unable to keep the blush from heating my cheeks. Thank God, Grady was too young to catch those subtle cues, but I needed to cool it with the humming. Every muscle in my body was deliciously sore, reminding me of the workout Nico had given me, and I couldn't stop smiling. I'd managed a quick shower before Grady woke up, needing the private time to put my head on straight, but I was still turned around and twisted up inside in the most wonderful way.

As if hearing my internal dialogue, Nico appeared, adorably rumpled from sleep and sexy as ever. *Did the man ever have an off day?* Didn't seem fair to the rest of the mere mortals in the world.

To Nico, I said, "Good morning," and returned to seeking out cereal or something, but in truth, I was trying not to appear as if anything had changed between us.

But something had changed.

I couldn't deny it. My body was in tune with his in a way that I'd never imagined possible.

Don't get me wrong, I'd enjoyed good sex before, but what'd happened between Nico and I had been beyond good—it'd been...life-altering.

So, pretending it hadn't happened...well, that was easier said than done, but I had to find a way because I wasn't about to let Grady think that Nico was going to be a permanent part of our life.

He squinted against the morning sunlight and rasped, "Are you looking for anything in particular?"

"Breakfast cereal?"

"I don't eat cereal."

"That would explain why I can't find any. No worries, I'll just make toast with peanut butter for Grady, then."

"Do you like that?" Nico asked Grady before reaching for the coffeepot to start brewing.

"It's okay," Grady admitted. "I like pancakes better."

Nico looked to me with a grin. "Then he should have pancakes."

I graced Nico with an indulgent look but said, "We don't have time to make pancakes. Grady has school this morning."

Grady immediately started protesting, "But Nico said we were going sailing today!"

"Well, Nico probably didn't realize that you had school. You can go sailing another time," I said, but I hated the crestfallen expression on my little son's face. How could spending the morning learning the ABCs possibly compare with the open ocean, especially given Grady was already way ahead of his classmates and was most times bored in class. But I had to adhere to structure, so I held the course. "Come on, let's get dressed while your bread is toasting. We have to leave a little earlier to make it on time."

Apparently, Nico was also destroyed by Grady's sad expression and said, "How about a compromise? We sail after school? We can still get in a few hours of quality time on the ocean in the afternoon."

Grady brightened with hope. "Really?"

"Of course. To be honest, I'm usually never awake this early so I often sail in the afternoon."

"Do you have your own sailboat?" Grady asked, his eyes shining.

"I do and it's been too long since I've taken her out. She deserves a little time away from the dock. So here's the deal, you go to school, your mom and I will do a little work, and then afterward, we'll pick you up and hit the water. Deal?"

"That's a deal and a half!" Grady hit an exuberant high five with Nico, and my heart stuttered. I wasn't sure if I was comfortable with how easily Nico had my kid wrapped so tightly around his finger, but I loved seeing Grady so happy. To be honest, most days Grady was such a serious soul, it felt good to see him act his age.

Grady scrambled to the bedroom to dress, and I turned to Nico to whisper, "Careful making promises to a six-year-old. They have a memory like an elephant and they will not let you forget."

But instead of heeding my warning, Nico said,

"Good. We all need an accountability partner from time to time," and I was both awed and fearful of what was happening.

"We are truly going to work, right?" I asked him before Grady returned.

"Sure," he answered, but the glint in his eye made me shiver. "But I didn't say how I was going to work you."

My breath hitched in my throat. I should've shut him down, reminded him that I was here to do a job and that had to be the priority, but my body was still tingling with the aftereffects of what he'd done to me, and I wanted more.

Heaven help me, I wanted more.

I swallowed and dragged my gaze away from the hunger in his, nearly jumping when the toast popped from the toaster. Nico chuckled, knowing where my head was at, but he did me the courtesy of remaining silent as he poured two cups of coffee and slid mine over to me wordlessly. I spread a generous helping of peanut butter on the toast and grabbed a short glass of milk before I could risk meeting Nico's gaze again.

"Thank you," I murmured, lifting the coffee mug, my thoughts stubbornly returning to the memory of last night. Grady returned, looking like a million bucks, if a million bucks wore its shirt inside out and both shoes on the wrong feet. "Baby." I chuckled, going to help him straighten himself out. "One of these days you're going to have to learn your right from your left shoe."

"But they look the same to me," Grady complained with a frown.

Nico chuckled and grabbed a permanent marker

from a drawer. "C'mere, little man," he said, helping Grady onto the counter. Then he drew an R and an L on each respective shoe in an inconspicuous spot so it wasn't completely obvious. "There. Now you can just look for the R and L. Easy-peasy."

"Awesome! Mama never lets me draw on my shoes!"

I laughed, sobering slightly to say, "And I still don't, but we can let this one slide. Okay, now you have zero excuses. Eat your toast. We need to leave in about five minutes, and you still need to brush your teeth and wash the sleep from your eyes."

"Aw, Mama, you're always trying to make me fancy. I'm not trying to find a girlfriend yet, you know."

Nico guffawed at that and I chuckled, too. "Well, maybe I just don't want your poor teacher to catch a whiff of your dragon breath and faint."

Grady giggled but said, "Mrs. Tipper is the one with dragon breath. I think she brushes her teeth with dirt."

"Grady Erickson Hughes, you take that back," I admonished. "We don't talk about our teachers like that. Or anyone for that matter."

"Okay, Mama," Grady said but grinned when Nico gave him a conspiratorial wink. Good Lord, Nico was like a kid himself. Grady finished and headed for the bathroom, giving me a minute to scold Nico, but Nico had other plans.

"You—"

His mouth sealed against mine for a stolen kiss, and my knees threatened to buckle. Everything we'd done together last night came roaring back in full detail, and it took everything I had not to moan like a porn star on cue.

But before I embarrassed myself, Nico released me

and I spun out of his arms just in time for Grady to appear, face scrubbed, teeth brushed and ready to slay the dragons of kindergarten.

I may always question my judgment when it came to dating Houston, but we'd made a beautiful child together, and for that, I couldn't spare a moment of regret.

"Let's do this," I said, reaching for his hand.

"The car is downstairs waiting," Nico said, sinking into the sofa with his coffee in hand, a delicious grin on his sexy mug. "I can't wait to get to work when you return."

And by *work* I was fairly certain he meant something else entirely.

Funny thing, I was totally okay with that.

For now.

CHAPTER EIGHTEEN

Nico

MY BODY VIBRATED with anxious energy as I jumped into the shower, dressed and awaited Lauren's return. Last night had been an anomaly, and I was eager to see if it'd simply been the thrill of victory or something else entirely that caused me to react like an alien had taken over my brain.

I wasn't a cuddler by nature. I preferred my space. In fact, I was always the one biting my tongue in half after a hookup so I didn't ruin my chances of seeing the woman again by saying something rude such as, "That was great. The car is waiting downstairs to take you home."

But I hadn't wanted Lauren to leave. I'd wanted her right by my side. I wanted to feel my cock nestled against her backside, my arm wrapped tightly around her midsection.

But I hadn't been relieved at all. I'd been miffed.

Which was why I had to see if my reaction was a one-time event or something else. I needed firmer footing beneath me because right now, I felt as if the world had just tipped over and I was left standing on my head.

The door opened and Lauren returned. I could sense her nervousness, as well. The best way to handle a situation like this was to simply rip the bandage in one fell swoop. Without giving her a chance to think, I met her at the door and kissed her hard, demanding every ounce of her attention, every breath in her body.

Instant arousal burned through me, incinerating all the rational thought and careful planning in my head. All I knew was I needed to be inside Lauren again, and I wasn't about to wait.

However, Lauren was the one who managed to hold on to her senses long enough to gasp, "Wait!" pushing her hand against my chest, wrenching her mouth away.

I blinked away the haze of sexual fog to stare quizzically. "What's wrong?"

"I don't know…this feels…it's too intense. This can't be normal."

I couldn't agree more, which was why I needed to figure out why. I reached for the buttons on her blouse and began plucking them open. "Define normal," I suggested with silky intention, biting my lip on a groan as her breasts came into view. "Has anyone ever told you you have gorgeous tits?"

Lauren blushed, her breath catching. "Not lately."

"Well, they are." I pushed the halves of her open blouse from her shoulders and filled my hands with her full breasts. "A perfect handful—" adding with a look "—and a delicious mouthful." To demonstrate, I sucked a sweet, soft nipple into my mouth and suckled gently.

"Nico," she gasped, the sound like music to me.

I spent a little time on her other nipple, and after, I wasted no time in shucking my jeans to stand naked and ready. Lauren sank to her knees in front of me to nuzzle my cock, her reaction twisting me in knots with instant arousal.

"I love the smell of a man's body," she murmured, cupping my balls with tender care before bringing the head of my cock straight to her mouth. I fed my shaft down her throat, and she willingly took every inch, teasing me with her tongue and adding a zing of danger with the graze of her teeth. Her hands worked in tandem with her mouth, sliding up and down my shaft as she worked the head with her mouth. Before long, my legs were shaking and sweat beaded my brow as I got ready to blow.

"I'm going to come," I said from between gritted teeth, trying to hold back, but Lauren didn't back away. She wanted me to come in her mouth. That was the final straw. I broke loose, coming with a shout, my knees nearly buckling and sending me sprawling to the sofa. With a final swipe of her tongue against the ultrasensitive head, she grinned up at me as I rested against the wall, breathing hard.

Lauren rose, went to the kitchen and grabbed a bottled water from the fridge. Then she drank deep before sinking down onto the sofa. I joined her and she offered me a drink, which I gladly slugged down. "Give me a minute," I promised, my throat still dry from breathing so heavily. "Girl, you've got some skills on lock."

Lauren laughed, taking the compliment for what it was—genuine—and actually reached for her notebook. "I thought we'd go over some notes, maybe come up with a framework for your autobiography so we can figure out how to structure the book."

Was she really talking about business? *Oh, hell no.* I tugged the notebook from her fingers, ignoring her mild protest, and tossed it before reaching for her pants and yanking them free from her body. Lauren laughed as I parted her legs to feast on her lovely pussy. "We have to do some work," she said, trying to close her legs, but I wasn't having it. I hadn't had my breakfast yet.

"Oh, I told you I planned to work you," I said, grinning. "By the time I'm finished with your body, you're going to have to walk bowlegged to the kitchen to make me a sandwich."

Lauren pealed with laughter until I buried my face between her slick folds, eager to reacquaint myself with the unique taste of her sweet pussy. I was a quick study. Within moments I had her dialed in. I knew just where to push, press, lick and suck to have her twisting and arching against my mouth, keening a cry so hoarse that I was sure my neighbors were going to lodge a noise complaint.

And I loved it.

Free to cut loose, Lauren did exactly that—the sound of her coming was the most erotic thing I'd ever encountered, and I wanted to bottle it up in my imagination so I could listen to it whenever I needed to stroke myself.

She shuddered and bucked, but I held her in place, locking her hips with my arms so I could tease and torture that swollen little nub. Ringing Lauren's bell had just catapulted to my No. 1 favorite pastime, and I never wanted to stop.

But after her third orgasm, Lauren weakly pushed at me, begging me to let her breathe. "Please, Nico... no more... *Ohhhhh, God!*" Another orgasm rattled her bones and she went limp, whimpering as the pleasure buffeted her on its way out.

I turned her loose and swiveled her around so that her ass was bent over the sofa, her face turned sidewise as she gasped for air. I ripped a condom open, tossed the packaging and quickly sheathed so I could drill her as hard as ever.

Her groan as I slowly entered her from behind was like gasoline on a fire. I pushed myself deep, going to the hilt, until I was buried inside her, her pussy clenching around me in slick, hot, welcome.

"Fuck, Lauren," I gasped. Now it was my turn to lose it. My eyes rolled back as I pumped against her, trying for finesse, but I was desperate to plant myself inside her. My hips worked furiously as I pounded against the soft give of her ass, and it didn't take long before I was coming, too.

I spent myself inside her until I was bone-dry. I slowly pulled out, careful to keep the condom from spilling, and tossed it before dropping to the floor, exhausted.

Lauren rolled to the floor to land beside me, her head rolling to the cushion. There was something so incredibly beautiful about her when she looked rode hard. Her hair was wild and her cheeks flushed. She wasn't wearing a stitch of makeup, and I'd never seen a woman more stunning.

"Why are you staring?" she asked, a rueful smile following as she tried to fix her hair. "I know I probably look like a crazy person."

"You look amazing," I said, reaching to pull her to me as I brushed a tender kiss across her lips. After the kiss, we simply held each other's stare, unsure of what was happening between us, both of us a little afraid to draw attention to it. "Are you hungry?" I asked, breaking the moment and climbing to my feet. "I was just kidding about the sandwich. I'll make us something."

Lauren reached for her panties and retrieved her blouse from the foyer, dressing quickly, much to my disappointment. I would've rather Lauren stayed naked. Easy access and an awesome view, if you asked me.

For myself, I remained naked.

"Ham and turkey panini?" I suggested, already moving to grab the fixings.

"Sounds good."

I made quick work of the panini and returned with the sandwiches.

"Are you going to get dressed?" she asked, accepting her plate, trying not to stare at my cock. "I mean... it might be a good idea."

"I like being naked."

She laughed. "I bet you do."

"Don't you?"

"I have a six-year-old son. Being naked isn't an option."

I shrugged. "He's not here now. Go ahead, be free, go naked."

Lauren laughed, her eyes sparkling. "But if I'm naked I have a feeling we won't get much work done, and we only have so much time before we have to pick up Grady and go sailing as you promised."

"Good point," I admitted, reaching for my pants. As

much as I wanted to fuck Lauren at least a few more times, I wasn't going to disappoint Grady by being late.

Dressed and enjoying our sandwiches, I couldn't help but wonder what the story behind Grady's father was. Lauren didn't like to talk about it, but my curiosity didn't much care about boundaries.

"Is Grady's dad dead?" I asked bluntly. "Is that why you don't like to talk about him?"

"He's not dead," Lauren answered. "Though that might make things easier. At least if he were dead, I wouldn't have to explain to Grady that his father had abandoned him without a second look."

"He knows about Grady?"

"Of course he does."

"Does he pay child support?"

Lauren looked at me sharply. "No, and I prefer it that way. If I don't chase after him for support, he's happy to leave us alone. Trust me, Grady is better off without his dad around."

"Who the hell is this guy?"

Lauren ignored my question, drawing attention to her sandwich. "This is pretty good. If the billionaire, independently wealthy gig doesn't pan out, you can always become a chef or at the very least a line cook."

"You deflect so quickly when you don't want to talk about a subject," I observed, amused. "So what happened between you and your baby daddy?"

"Please don't call him that," Lauren said, grimacing. "It was a humiliating time in my life and I just don't like to talk about it. Besides, Grady and I are a team, we don't need anyone else."

"Everyone needs someone," I reminded her softly, but she just shook her head, disagreeing.

"Nope. My son and I are a duo. We don't need a third wheel."

"How does Grady feel about that?"

Lauren shrugged, picking at her crust. "He hasn't said it bothers him. I assume because it's all he's ever known that he's fine with it."

"Kids are perceptive."

"Yes they are, and Grady can see how good things are, so why throw a wrench into things, you know?" She paused, adding with mild annoyance, "What does it matter to you? Are you trying to play matchmaker or something? Because I'm not interested in being with Grady's father under any circumstances."

"Is he that bad?" I asked, curious.

"He's not bad, he's just...very selfish. Trust me, Grady is better off without an influence like that."

Now I needed a name. I didn't understand how a man could walk away from his kid. Even though I wasn't hoping for a baby mama to show up out of the blue, I would certainly make an effort to be part of the child's life if one did. Besides, my mother would kill me if she found out she had a grandchild out there whom I'd abandoned.

My brother Luca and his new wife, Katherine, were about to add a new generation of Donatos to the mix with the birth of their first child in a month or two, and my mother was practically wetting herself with happiness at the prospect of becoming a *nonna*.

"What's his name?" I pressed, but Lauren wasn't interested in sharing and got up to put her plate away. I rose to follow her. "Is it a secret? Is that why you don't want to tell me?"

She glared. "It's not a secret, it's private." But then she exhaled loudly before adding with chagrin, "And there's a good chance you know him."

CHAPTER NINETEEN

Lauren

I HADN'T PLANNED to admit to Nico that there was a good possibility he knew Houston. The information just kinda fell from my mouth in an embarrassing word vomit.

"Now I have to know," he said. "Out with it. Who is this asshole who may or may not be within my circle?"

I sighed, unable to believe I'd been so careless. "Honestly, I don't want to tell you. We've spent the last six years living peacefully without his influence, and I don't need anyone to rock the boat."

"You don't think at some point this mystery man might decide he wants to be a father and sue for custody?"

I lifted my chin. "There's literally no reason why Grady's father would want to suddenly become involved in his son's life. He doesn't even know him. It would be a disaster and it would completely throw Grady's life out of whack. Trust me, it is better for everyone involved for his father to remain absent."

But Nico wasn't satisfied. He was like a dog with a bone. I never should've said anything. I sincerely regretted opening my mouth. "I've seen your shitty apartment. The man should at least be paying child support."

I hated this argument—it was the same argument my mom threw at me—and just as I said to her, I said to Nico, "It's none of your business. Back off."

Nico seemed to understand that he'd overstepped but nonetheless tried a different tack. "I know you don't want to hear this, but at some point Grady is going to want to know his father. It might be later when he's a teenager, but it will happen at some point. How are you prepared to deal with it?"

Like that wasn't one of my deepest fears already, but I couldn't live in fear of a moment that may or may not happen. "I guess I'll cross that bridge when I come to it. Right now Grady is six years old and completely happy with just him and me."

"And I'm not advocating that you suddenly invite this man into Grady's life, whoever this asshole is. I'm just pointing out that you're walking a tightrope and at some point someone might shake the line."

As much as I wanted to end the conversation and erase it from Nico's memory, I could sense that Nico wasn't going to let it go. If Nico truly wanted to find out who Grady's father was, he could easily do so with minimal effort because all he had to do was throw money at the mystery.

In an effort to avoid Nico poking around and inadvertently messing with the beehive, I decided to come clean, but not without scowling for putting his nose where it didn't belong.

"I'll tell you, but you have to promise me that you will not say anything to him or in any way encourage him to be a part of Grady's life, no matter how you feel about the subject. Do I have your word?"

"Of course."

I didn't know how strong or good Nico's word was, so I'd have to trust him. I drew a deep breath before sharing, "Grady's father is Houston Beaumont."

As expected, Nico's expression was one of shock. I knew they probably ran in the same circles. Houston was a rich asshole, too.

"I've never heard anything about Houston having a kid," he said. "That son of a bitch. What a dick."

I released a breath of relief. A part of me had been afraid that Nico might take Houston's side. A "bros before hoes" kind of thing, but Nico wasn't walking that road in this instance.

"So you and Houston were a thing?" he asked, obviously trying to picture that and failing. I didn't blame Nico; Houston and I had been an odd couple.

"Briefly," I admitted. "I'd thought I was in love with him, but he bailed when I was four months pregnant. He begged me not to say anything about the baby, which is why nobody in his circle knows about it. At first I thought he didn't want me to say anything because he wanted to make a grand announcement, but then I realized he didn't want anyone to know because he'd never had any plans of being a father. Once I realized that, I didn't want anything to do with him. I was going to raise my baby by myself, and I did."

"Houston comes from a very rich family," Nico said. "He might've been willing to simply pay child support and not have anything to do with the kid."

"That's a gamble I wasn't willing to take. You have to understand that once I saw Houston's true colors I didn't want him having a hand in raising my child. I felt stupid enough as it was that I'd been conned and knocked up by the man. I wasn't about to subject a newborn baby to his bullshit. Besides, Houston would've wanted to see his kid if he was paying money. Houston is very much possession-driven. He would've looked at Grady as nothing more than a possession, and frankly, there's no amount of money in this world that could make that okay with me. So Houston can go fuck himself."

I hadn't meant to reveal so much, but there was something about Nico that unhinged my jaw and the words simply fell out. Maybe it was something I'd needed to say for a long time and I'd finally found an ear willing to listen. Anytime the subject of Houston came up with my mom, she was a broken record. "Go after him for the money." It was the same thing over and over and over again, and I just didn't want to hear it anymore.

But Nico seemed to understand that Houston wasn't a great person to have coparenting a child.

Oddly, his support meant something to me. "How well do you know Houston?" I asked, curious.

"Well enough. We went to school together. He's an asshole but in certain circumstances fun to have around. However, I wouldn't consider him an actual friend by any means."

"Well, like I said, I've been lucky to this point in that Houston has had zero interest in having anything to do with us. I haven't pressed for child support, and he's been happy to forget that we exist. We don't travel in the same circles, and it's not likely that Houston is going to run into Grady anytime soon or vice versa."

"That's true enough. Have you ever considered asking Houston if he would terminate his parental rights and just be done with it? That way the threat of him popping in whenever he feels like it is removed."

Actually, I had thought of that option. But at the time I couldn't afford an attorney to draw the paperwork, and again, there was always the risk that poking at the issue might ignite some weird need to press the other direction. "I couldn't fathom the risk of losing Grady. If we went to court for custody, the odds were stacked against me. Even though I'm his mother, the judge could've taken one look at Houston's wealth and my meager means and given custody to the father. Houston would've pawned off Grady to some nanny—one he probably would've been screwing—and Grady would've been shuffled off into the background. I wasn't about to take that chance."

"Fair enough. But you have the money now. Payment was wired to your bank this morning. If you want to check your bank balance, you can. You have more than enough to hire a good attorney if you ever wanted to press Houston to terminate his rights."

My breath caught. I'd forgotten about the payment. I didn't want to rush to my phone to check my bank balance but... I looked at Nico, biting my lip with indecision. "Are you sure, I'd really like to check to see if it's really there."

He chuckled and gestured for me to go ahead. I picked up the phone and checked my bank balance. I nearly choked on my own tongue when I saw how many zeros were in my bank account. I looked at him, still stunned. "I can't believe you actually paid me that much money. It's too much. I feel like I'm taking advantage."

"The fact that you're worried tells me that you wouldn't know how to take advantage of someone if you tried. It's not in your nature. People who take advantage of others don't think twice about it. And honestly, you're worth it."

I couldn't help but warm under his praise. I didn't even care if he meant it was for my writing skills or the fact that we clicked together really well in bed. All that mattered was everything that I'd ever worried about financially was over. I could pay off all my debt—which included two student loans—as well as put money aside for a nest egg. One of the worst things I suffered was the knowledge that I never had enough money left over after each pay period to put aside for a rainy day fund, something my dad had drilled into me since I was twelve. But I'd just made a year's salary for a month's work, and as long as I found a permanent job after, I could.

My eyes brimming with tears, I turned to Nico. "Thank you. You have no idea how money like that has the ability to change someone's life."

Nico shifted with discomfort. "Don't be getting all sappy on me. It's nothing."

"But it is something to me. I understand that you were raised with wealth and this is probably pennies to you, but to me it's everything. And I'm going to work my ass off to prove to you that it was money well spent."

He surprised me with a quick but gentle kiss. "Baby, whatever happens from this point forward I already feel that it was money well spent. I meant what I said when I told you I liked you and Grady. You're both cool people, and in my life finding genuine people is difficult at best. If this helps you work out the kinks in your life, I'm happy to do so."

I couldn't stop the tears this time. I'd sorely misjudged Nico in so many ways. I was ashamed of my judgment and how I'd been such a bitch when we first met. But I could change that. I would absolutely do my best to write his autobiography and do him justice. I didn't know what his beef was with his brother, but I sensed that no one truly saw Nico for who he was.

And I would do my best to draw an accurate portrait with my words.

Sensing the moment was becoming too deep, Nico wiped my tears and helped me to stand. "I say we rinse off, fuck in the shower, rinse off again and then go get Grady to go sailing. Are you down?"

I nodded. "I'm so down."

"All right, then," he said, sealing his mouth to mine for another lingering kiss. "Let's do this. We're on a time crunch."

CHAPTER TWENTY

Nico

FROM THE OUTSIDE looking in, my sailboat wasn't the fanciest, but that's what I liked about the Celestial 48. I'd bought it used and then spent a year overhauling it, customizing the interior with rich teak and shiny chrome fixtures. The *Nauti Kitty* was my sweet mistress that I didn't spend nearly enough time with, and yet she still purred like a kitten whenever I took her out.

"Whoa!" Grady exclaimed as I helped him and his mom onto the deck. "This is awesome! You own this boat?"

"Down to every bolt and barnacle," I answered with a grin, loving how Grady's eyes sparkled with excitement. I'd forgotten how exhilarating it could be to enjoy something through someone else's eyes. My friends always mocked my little boat, saying I was the only billionaire who preferred to slum it when I could afford a luxury yacht ten times over, but there was something about this boat that I'd been drawn to.

Granted, the purchase had been on a whim. A drunken whim, at that, but I hadn't regretted my decision, not even when I'd sobered up and seen how much work it needed.

"When I bought her, she'd been in sorry shape, but fixing her up has been more fun than I ever imagined it would be. Gave me the opportunity to make her mine."

Lauren agreed with Grady and was similarly awed. "I think she's gorgeous."

My smile deepened. Somehow Lauren's praise meant so much more than anyone else's. "Let me give you a tour before we hit the open water," I said, motioning for them to follow me below deck. The accommodations were cozy, but then, I wasn't accustomed to bringing too many people here. Grady wandered from the galley to the head to the two staterooms, poking his head in each to give a nod of approval after his inspection.

"I like it," he announced. "I think I could live here."

Lauren laughed. "I'm not living on a boat," she said, letting him down gently. "But it is very pretty."

"That she is," I agreed. I pulled a life jacket from a small supply closet and buckled Grady in. "Here's the deal, little man. Anyone under the age of thirteen has to wear one of these if they're going to be above deck. No exceptions, got it?"

Grady nodded solemnly. "Yes, sir."

I chucked his chin playfully. "That's 'Yes, Captain,' sailor. Got it?"

Grady grinned and giggled. "Yes, Captain!"

"Excellent." To Lauren, I said, "If you'd like to wear a life vest, you're welcome to, I have all sizes available right here. It's up to you."

"Are you a good driver or...um, sailor?"

I laughed. "I haven't capsized yet so I take that as a good sign."

Lauren grabbed a vest. "Just in case."

I chuckled and we climbed back to the top, where Lauren and Grady settled into the bench seats, soaking up the sun, while I got the *Nauti Kitty* ready for launch.

The day was gorgeous, perfect for sailing. The wind picked up nicely, and by the time we'd maneuvered out of the dock and hit the open waters, we were on wind power alone and clipping along at a nice leisurely pace.

Because he was interested, I gave Grady a quick lesson on nautical terms.

I felt rather than saw Lauren's attention on Grady and me. I cast her a quick look, and she smiled with a subtle blush at being caught. There was something happening between us that felt different from anything I'd ever experienced.

I didn't know what it was—but it scared me as much as it was exhilarating. I'd been hoping for a new adventure, something to break up the monotony that'd become my life, but I realized as I ruffled Grady's sandy-blond hair that I may have bitten off more than I'd planned.

My thoughts were consumed with Lauren and Grady at all times. I wanted to curl up with Lauren and explore each other's bodies as much as I wanted to show Grady the wonders of the world just waiting to be discovered if one had the resources to make it happen.

"Have you ever been outside of New York?" I asked Grady.

He looked to Lauren. "Have I, Mama?"

She shook her head. "Traveling takes time and

money, sweetheart. Good thing for us, there are lots of awesome things to see and do in New York City."

I smiled but the world was so much bigger than one state could possibly hope to provide. "The resource part shouldn't be too much of an obstacle now," I said to Lauren with a wink, but she just laughed. "You ought to take a trip to Europe. My family is from Tuscany. Italy is a place everyone should see at least once."

"Well, after I pay off my student loans and put money away for savings, there won't be a lot left over to traipse around the world, but maybe someday."

I frowned. "Do you need more money?"

"No, not at all. I'm completely satisfied with the amount agreed upon," she said, shaking her head. "I just have different priorities, and running off to Italy isn't one of them, unfortunately."

I wanted Lauren and Grady to see where my roots came from, but I supposed that wasn't my place to insist. Hell, I'd even pay for the entire trip, but again, I was wandering into territory that was strewn with tacks and broken glass—and best avoided.

I set the course and Grady helped me steer while Lauren went down to the galley to fix some sandwiches.

"Did your dad teach you to sail?" Grady asked, his little body in front of mine while we cruised along.

I chuckled. "Nope. My dad didn't have time for sailing. I had a lot of time to fill in my childhood, so I found ways to keep myself occupied. I'd always been fascinated by sailboats, so when the opportunity arose, I snagged it. The old man I bought the *Nauti Kitty* from taught me to sail. He was a crusty old fart, but he knew his stuff. Best damn teacher ever." I paused for a moment, before adding, "Unfortunately, he died a year after I bought the boat."

"Why?"

Liver failure. The man had been a raging alcoholic, but I softened the truth by answering, "He got sick and it was more than his old body could handle."

"That's a bummer."

"Agreed."

"The *Nauti Kitty* was a good buy," Grady said with firm approval. "As Mama would say, it was a bargain!"

I laughed. "How do you know? I might've overpaid. My friends say I should've got it for free and then given it a good burial at sea."

"That's dumb. This boat is fab."

"Fab?"

"That's what Uncle Ronnie says when he likes something."

I nodded. "I agree. The *Nauti Kitty* is fab."

We cruised along in amiable silence until Grady said, "Do you like my mama? 'Cuz I think she likes you."

My tongue felt glued to my palate. I had to tread cautiously. I didn't want Grady getting hurt by anything I might inadvertently set in motion, but I wasn't being dishonest when I answered, "Hell yes. She's pretty cool. Kinda cute, too, but don't let her know that. I wouldn't want her to get a big head or else she won't fit in the narrow corridors below deck."

Grady giggled and I warmed at the sweet sound. "She likes you a lot."

"Yeah? And how do you know?" I asked, curious.

"Because she looks at you funny."

"Ah, the telltale funny look. Maybe she thinks I smell?"

"Not that kind of funny look," Grady said, laughing as he twisted to illustrate, "this kind of funny look."

I guffawed at the googly eyes Grady was making on his mom's behalf. "Boy, I must be blind because I've never seen that particular look on your mama's face."

I'd seen her eyes roll up into her skull as I made her come and I'd seen her eyes squeeze shut with total pleasure as I bent her in half, but I'd never seen those googly eyes.

Grady nodded with the confidence of a six-year-old who already knew his letters and how to write his name, saying, "Yep. She does," and who was I to argue?

"I'll bet it's fun just being you and your mom all the time," I said, fishing for a little intel. "No one to share your mom with or tag-team for extra TV privileges, right?"

Grady shrugged. "I guess."

"You guess?"

"Well, most times. I like when we have movie night. She makes kettle corn and orders pizza. She even lets me drink soda on those special nights, but I overheard Auntie Claire tell Mama that if she doesn't get a man soon her *angina* was going to fall off."

I nearly fell over from laughing so hard. "Her angina? Sounds serious," I said when I managed to catch my breath.

"I know! I don't know what that is, but I don't want my mama to lose anything just because my real dad is a jerk face and doesn't want to be with her and me.

Can you help my mama find a boyfriend so that doesn't happen?"

The earnest request was so sweet that I almost readily applied for the job until I caught my mouth before making an ass of myself. I wasn't boyfriend material. I was a commitment-phobe with an insatiable appetite for the new and undiscovered. I would only break this little family into pieces, but I didn't want Grady worrying about his mom's parts so I said, "Don't worry about your mom. She's one tough cookie and I don't think she's in danger of anything falling off, okay?"

Grady seemed relieved and I resisted the urge to kiss the crown of his head. He was such a great kid. How could Houston not want to be a part of his son's life? I couldn't possibly picture Lauren and Houston together—and I didn't want to—but Houston never should've abandoned his son just because things didn't work out between him and Lauren.

Lauren called out from below deck, saying the sandwiches were ready. I lowered the sails, dropped the anchor so we could enjoy lunch on the calm waters and headed below deck with Grady.

Just as we slid into the bench-style seats at the small table, Grady assured his mom, "You don't have to worry, Mama. Nico says your *angina* is going to be just fine even if you don't get a boyfriend," and I wanted to slide under the table and die.

Right after I quit laughing.

CHAPTER TWENTY-ONE

Lauren

I WAS MORTIFIED to my toes, but Nico's laugh was infectious, especially when Grady was beaming at me as if he'd single-handedly solved all my problems.

"You two seem to be partners in crime," I said, shooting Nico a look as I shook my head. I knew I should've put a stop to whatever was happening between Nico and Grady, but sue me, was it wrong to let my kid enjoy some traditional male energy? I mean, I loved Ronnie from his glittery fingernails to his diva updo, but sometimes I wondered if Grady needed a break from the things Uncle Ronnie accidentally let slip.

Like learning how Uncle Ronnie's boy parts never showed through the shiny, skintight dress that he wore for his act.

But Grady sure seemed to like Nico. Perhaps more than was healthy. I'd always assumed that because he never talked about not having a dad around that he really didn't notice or care.

Maybe I'd been naive to think his silence meant he

was unobservant. Honestly, I should've known better—Grady noticed *everything*.

Finished with lunch, we headed back up top and while Grady helped Nico take the helm, I stretched out on the comfy bench seats, content to let the wind ruffle my hair and the sun warm my face.

The ocean was calm and the winds light. It was a perfect day in so many ways.

A subtle pulling in my chest reminded me that Grady wasn't the only one who needed to remember that this was all temporary. Nico wasn't looking to sign on for the long haul, and I didn't want Nico in that capacity either.

I smiled ruefully to myself at my own meandering thoughts. Nico, as a father? He was like a giant kid himself. My gaze drifted to Nico and Grady, and that subtle pull deepened to something far stronger. Nico was really good with Grady and Grady thought Nico was the cat's meow.

As if hearing my thoughts, Nico swiveled his gaze toward mine, that sexy smile sending ripples of excitement in its wake. *Hot potato, he's delicious.* I bit back a shy smile, afraid he might be about to read my thoughts with a single shot of that hot stare.

But Nico just grinned, his dimple flashing, and returned to teaching Grady the ropes about sailing when it was likely Grady would never have the opportunity to sail on a boat like this again as it wasn't exactly within my budget.

"So, I have this dinner thing I have to attend," Nico said, surprising me. "And I'd like you to go with me."

"What kind of dinner thing?" I asked, curious.

He shrugged. "The usual kind—pretentious food

and even more pretentious people—but it would make an interesting chapter in my book."

"How so?"

"Well, seeing as my brothers, Luca and Dante, handle the actual business operations, usually I get thrown the appearances when a Donato is required for networking."

"You're the face of the Donato company?" Lauren asked.

"Well, to a point."

I laughed but shook my head. "I wouldn't know what to wear or how to act. I'm not sure I would be your best choice for a date."

"And what if you're the only choice I want?" he said, stunning me with his counter.

All jokes aside, Nico was serious. He wanted me to be his date? "What if I get in the way of your networking?" I asked, and by networking, I meant something else entirely.

Nico didn't pretend to miss my meaning. "As I said, I only want you."

Stop it, I wanted to growl, because my heart was fluttering dangerously like that of a lovesick idiot and I didn't need the heartache of rejection or betrayal later down the road when everything went sour or when Nico decided he was finished with whatever game he was playing. "I don't have anything to wear," I said, hoping my excuse ended his interest, but I should've known better.

"Tell me your favorite color and I'll have ten dresses delivered for you to consider."

Grady piped up. "Mama's favorite color is vanilla, like the ice cream." *The little coconspirator.*

"Thank you, little man," Nico said, smiling down at Grady in a way that made my heartbeat quicken. "Vanilla it is."

And just like that, in Nico's mind it was settled—I was going to be his plus-one.

I should've protested more vehemently, putting my foot down, but a part of me didn't want to. I was intrigued by the idea of attending a dinner on Nico's arm, not as the reporter skimming the edges of the room, watching body language and keeping an ear open for possible juicy news I could spin into a story.

I was going as his ghostwriter, and based on what he'd just said, his date. Maybe this once, I'd just enjoy the moment. It wasn't often that a billionaire wanted to treat you to a night out dressed to the nines.

"Fine," I said, closing my eyes to simply enjoy what was left of the day. I didn't want to think anymore, or worry, or wonder.

The sun started to dip low in the sky, and Nico turned the boat around to head back to the harbor. There was enough of a bite in the air that Grady and I headed below deck to wrap up in a blanket.

As I snuggled my sweet boy, loving how his hair smelled of ocean air and happiness, I kissed the top of his head, privately smiling to myself. "Did you have fun today?" I asked.

"The best, Mama," Grady answered, and I could hear the smile in his tone. "Nico says we can take the boat out whenever we want as long as the weather is good."

I bit my lip, tempted to gently correct Grady but decided to leave it alone. No sense in ruining a great day with reality. "It sounded like Nico was teaching you all about sailing. I never knew you were into sail-boats that much."

"I love sailboats, Mama, but it's not like one would fit in our yucky apartment so I didn't say anything."

"Our apartment is not yucky," I admonished while rocking him gently. "We love our apartment. It's our home."

"It smells and there're bugs," Grady said. "Can we move? Nico says we should, and I think he's right."

"Well, Nico has his opinion but we have to get back to our life at some point, and I'm sure Nico will be ready to have his spare bedroom back."

"Nico doesn't care. He said if I wanted I could deco-rate the room any way I like. He said he has an interior decorator who could do whatever I want within a day."

"That's silly," I said, troubled by Nico's promises. "There's no point in redecorating a room that we're only going to be in temporarily."

Grady shrugged. "Nico says it's no big deal. He'll just change it back when we leave."

I supposed that was true. Nico was fairly noncha-lant about throwing money around, but I didn't think it was healthy for Grady to assume that money grew on Donato trees.

"How about this…when we get back home, we'll give your room a makeover. Fresh coat of paint, any color you like, and we'll work together on a theme. It'll be a fun project for us."

"Can Nico help?"

Okay, this was going too far. Grady was obviously too enamored with Nico for my comfort. I gently turned Grady to face me. "Honey, I know Nico is lots of fun and he's been super nice to us, but as soon as I finish the job our lives will return to normal, and normal doesn't include Nico."

Grady's expression darkened as his little face screwed into a frown. "I don't want to go back to life without Nico."

"Well, I can't do anything about that," I said frankly. "Nico isn't part of our family."

"He could be."

Frustrated by my inability to communicate to Grady what I was trying to say, I just exhaled and let it go. "We'll talk about it later. You're tired and getting grouchy. You need dinner, a bath and then bed. It's been a busy day."

Grady folded his arms across his chest, still scowling. "I'm not tired. You're just changing the subject. Auntie Claire says that's called *defecting*."

Oh, Auntie Claire. I am going to duct tape your mouth shut one of these days. I cleared my throat and tried to smile as I corrected Grady. "Actually, the word you're looking for is *deflecting*, and I'm not doing that, I'm simply stating facts. Besides, that conversation was over."

"But I still want to talk about it."

"Sorry. I'm pulling rank. Conversation over."

I thought Grady might argue some more, but he seemed to get the hint that I wasn't going to budge.

It was dark by the time we were back to the apartment, and in spite of his protests, Grady was asleep against Nico's shoulder. Thankfully, I'd foreseen this problem and had Grady eat on the boat while we made it back to the dock, but I wouldn't be able to give him a bath as I'd hoped.

I went to take my son from Nico's arms, but he

waved me away and took Grady to the bedroom himself. He laid Grady gently on the bed and, after removing his shoes, tucked him into bed.

Fully clothed.

"He needs pajamas," I told Nico, shaking my head with a small smile at how clueless Nico truly was around kids, but it was cute how he'd tried. I made quick work of getting Grady into pajamas and within minutes he was snuggled deep into the blankets, dead to the world.

I found Nico in the kitchen throwing together a small cheese and cracker platter to share with a bottle of wine he had decanted.

I was hungry but I knew the wine would just knock me out. "I'm exhausted," I admitted, selecting a wedge of cheese and a cracker to munch. "I think I'll just shower and head to bed. Thanks for the awesome day."

But Nico wasn't going to let me slink off, and I think a part of me knew that. He grasped my hand and pulled me to him. "I've waited all day to taste those lips again and I'm not going to bed without it."

I sank against him, his lips finding mine. There was something so perfect about the way we fit together—as if I were coming home after a long journey—and I was just as eager to sink into the familiar.

"How about I draw a bath for the two of us?" he suggested. "I'll wash your back, you wash mine?"

His suggestion was cute, but I already knew that if our naked bodies were in close proximity, we were having sex at some point and I was so tired I could barely keep my eyes open.

Although a bath sounded fantastic, I thought we both could use some distance. I needed to remind myself that Nico wasn't part of my future and it was foolhardy to pretend otherwise, especially when Grady was already too attached.

"Tempting," I said, pulling away. "But I think I'll just go to bed."

Nico frowned but nodded. I could tell he had more he wanted to say, but he didn't and I was grateful. I didn't have the energy to explain what was going through my head, especially when I sensed that Nico wasn't going to see things my way.

I closed the bedroom door softly behind me and exhaled a long breath. Even though fatigue dragged on my bones, a sense of emptiness went deeper. Nico and I had had sex this morning, but my body ached to feel him inside me, even if it were only a quickie.

See? This is a problem.

When the idea of climbing into bed with Nico and falling asleep in his arms sounded like heaven...yeah, that was a big problem.

Seemed Grady wasn't the only one skipping past the warning signs, headed straight for the chasm of heartbreak.

Stripping down to a T-shirt, I climbed into bed next to Grady and pressed a soft kiss on his forehead before snuggling down to close my eyes.

Careful, Lauren...you're about to fall—hard.

Or maybe I already had.

CHAPTER TWENTY-TWO

Nico

I WAS NERVOUS.

I adjusted my cuff links for the tenth time in as many minutes. Lauren hadn't come out of the bedroom yet.

Did she hate the dress? I'd personally picked out the style, but what if it wasn't to her liking? I would've rather taken her with me so she could model each selection, but I knew she'd never agree and I wasn't about to risk our date.

Grady was with his grandmother—a decision Lauren agonized over to the point that she almost backed out—and tonight I was going to show Lauren what it was like to be pampered.

If she ever comes out of the bedroom, that is.

My heart leaped into my throat as the door slowly opened and Lauren stepped out tentatively as if she had something to worry about.

I lost my ability to breathe.

"You're fucking stunning," I said, my voice trembling in an unmanly fashion. I cleared my throat and tried again, saying, "Truly stunning."

And that was an understatement. The soft vanilla
floor-length gown was a sumptuous complement to her
olive skin tone, and her chocolate-brown eyes made me
melt a little inside. I hurried to unclasp the jewelry box
in my shaking hands to reveal the glittering diamond
necklace I'd procured from the family jeweler, holding
my breath as Lauren gasped with wonder.

"Are you kidding me? Are those real?"

"Very. So please don't lose it," I teased as I carefully lifted the necklace to place around her neck and
clasped it into place. Her hand fluttered to the brilliant stones, and I saw her fingers tremble slightly.
I grazed the tender column of her neck, murmuring,
"That necklace could fund a small country, but it looks
perfectly at home on you."

Lauren graced me with a shy smile that sent bolts
of arousal straight to my cock, and I had to rein in
my desire to mess up her hair and makeup by bend-
ing her over the kitchen table before we left. "I don't
know what to say...this is too much but I'm so flattered. Thank you, Nico."

I swallowed the lump of pride in my throat. If anyone should be flattered, it was me. I was going to be
the luckiest son of a bitch in the room with Lauren on
my arm. Speaking of, I gallantly extended my arm for
her gloved hand to grasp. "Shall we?"

"We shall." She smiled, her brown eyes sparkling.

Tonight I'd called for a limousine rather than the
town car because I wanted Lauren to feel like Cinder-
ella and that I was her prince, but I also wanted more
privacy than the town car could provide.

Her smile deepened as she saw the awaiting stretch.
Jepperson opened the door with a deep bow and an ap-

preciative "Very beautiful," and helped Lauren into the car. I stuffed a hundred-dollar bill into his hand with a grin and he winked. "Y'all have a good time. I won't wait up."

As the door closed behind me, I leaned back to admire the beauty next to me. How could I have ever missed that delicate bone structure, that stubbornly beautiful intellect shining in her eyes? I must've been blind to believe Lauren plain in any way.

Lauren marveled quietly at the luxury, running her fingers lightly down the soft, black leather, smiling with excitement. "I've never ridden in a limo before."

"And? What do you think?"

"It doesn't suck."

I laughed at her dry humor. Then I said, "I have a surprise for you."

Her eyes widened. "A surprise? Oh, Nico, you've already done way too much..."

I chuckled but this surprise was also a selfish one. "These dinners are notoriously dull, but I think I've found a way to liven things up."

She frowned, curious as I fished my surprise from my interior jacket pocket. Lauren inhaled sharply, her hand flying to her mouth in shock as she said, "Is that...a...oh my God, what is that?"

I held in my hand a small, egg-shaped vibrator and the accompanying remote.

"And just what do you plan to do with that?" she asked, amused.

"I plan," I said, leaning forward to brush my lips across her mouth, "to ever so lovingly place this sweet little torture device inside that delicious pussy of yours so that when I feel things are becoming dull, I'll give it a discreet little flick. The fun part will be watching you squirm knowing there's nothing you can do to stop the pleasure."

"You're the devil," she said, but her mouth curved in a delighted smile. I kissed her harder until she was panting and squirming, the heat between us building quickly. My hand found itself up her gown to discover her without panties. She blushed but her brow rose in challenge. A challenge I readily accepted and that made my cock hard. I used her slick wetness to ease the egg past her soft folds and deep inside. I withdrew and slowly licked her wetness from my fingers. She shuddered in response, her gaze as liquid as her slit.

"Shall we test this sucker out?" I asked, grinning though my cock was already threatening to burst through my pants. She nodded and I flicked the remote, giving her a nice zing. She gasped and gripped the armrest, her cheeks flushing prettily. "Very nice," I said with approval. "At least we know it works."

Lauren laughed, the sound like music to me, and I couldn't help but kiss her again. At this rate, I'd never make it through dinner without needing to fuck her senseless, but I'd give it a good college try.

She shocked me by saying in a throaty tone, "Let me suck your cock," and I couldn't get my pants down fast enough. My cock sprang free and she was on it within a heartbeat. I closed my eyes with pleasure as her hot mouth worked my cock and her hands cupped my balls, squeezing gently. I groaned, loving the feel of Lauren's mouth on me, losing myself to the bliss of a killer blowjob. I didn't want to make a mess on her beautiful dress, but when I tried to make her stop before I blew, she just giggled and kept going.

How could I *not* come so hard with a woman who clearly loved sucking cock like Lauren did?

Yeah, exactly.

With a guttural grunt, I found my release. Lauren swallowed every drop until I was left gasping for air and nearly springing from my seat from a single teasing swipe of her tongue across the ultrasensitive pulsing head of my cock.

"I think you might be the devilish one," I said when I could speak again. To that she just laughed, and I gave the remote a flick, sending a pleasurable bolt straight to her tingly bits.

"That's one powerful little egg," she said with a breathy moan that would've made me instantly hard if I hadn't just blown a wad. "Oh, God...that feels good."

Sadly, we'd arrived at our destination and it was time to be adults. I laughed and pocketed the remote in my interior pocket, patting it with a wink. "Just in case things get dull," I promised, but she and I both knew it was going to be a challenge for me to keep my hands off the remote for the entire night because I loved watching her cheeks flush with pleasure.

And the fact that only she and I knew what was happening was an incredible turn-on.

Not that I needed anything else to turn me on when it came to Lauren. Jesus, at this point, I think watching her brush her teeth would probably cause my dick to harden.

The driver opened our door, and once I climbed out, I helped Lauren, her hand slipping into mine as if it were always meant to be there.

Pride warmed my insides as I caught enviable

glances from the other guests, everyone's tongues wagging at the mysterious stranger on my arm.

But to be honest, it wouldn't have mattered if only Lauren and I were attending this function and there were no other people to admire what a beauty I'd snagged—I didn't care what anyone else thought.

"With Fort Knox on my chest, you might need to hire more security," Lauren murmured, glancing with obvious nervousness around her.

"You're safe with me," I assured her and she relaxed.

We entered the ballroom filled wall-to-wall with people in designer dresses and tuxedos, and I felt Lauren's nervousness through the thin sheath of her dress. "People are bound to stare. Keep your head high. You're the most beautiful woman in the room."

"How can you say that?" she whispered. "I think I just saw Gwyneth Paltrow in the corner!"

I shrugged. "She pales in comparison to you, and I'm not just saying that. I mean it, Lauren. You are exquisite—and not just because that dress clings to your every curve. It's because you're something these women could never hope to be."

"Yeah? And what's that?" she asked, dubious.

"Genuine."

A smile broke through her nerves. "You're really charming when you put your mind to it," she said, drawing a little bit closer to me. "You ought to write a book on how to charm the pants off women. I'm sure it would be a bestseller."

I chuckled but there was only one woman I wanted naked at the moment, and she was gracing my arm.

I took two flutes of champagne from a passing attendant and handed one to Lauren with a small toast.

"To an evening filled with surprises…" Lauren smiled and we clinked glasses softly before sipping and surveying the room. I spied plenty of people I wanted to avoid for various reasons, but mostly I wanted to find an empty room, lift Lauren's skirt around her hips and remind her why we were so good together.

But if I couldn't do that…I supposed I ought to go and network for the sake of Donato Inc. After all, sailboats didn't pay for themselves, and this was how I earned my play money.

CHAPTER TWENTY-THREE

Lauren

I WAS A fairy princess and Nico was my dirty prince.

We floated across the dance floor, laughing and smiling as if we were the only two people in the world until Nico flicked the tiny remote and I nearly stumbled into his arms, clinging to him as my body shuddered with pleasure. I clung to Nico, inhaling sharply as I tried not to moan, and he simply chuckled with wicked delight as I struggled to maintain my composure.

He released the trigger and I nipped at his neck before allowing him to release me. Nico rewarded me with a feral growl that I felt down to my toes.

It was intensely erotic, and I couldn't stop smiling.

We suffered the obligatory small talk when Nico's presence was required, and after we'd circulated the room enough times, we slipped out of the ballroom and down a quiet hallway, surreptitiously trying doors for one that wasn't locked.

Nico found one and we slipped inside, quietly locking the door behind us.

The room, an office with ornate furnishings inlaid

with gilt filigree, was entirely too gaudy for my tastes but I hardly cared about our surroundings. There was one reason and one reason only to be locked in a room with Nico in the dark while the rest of the party prattled on about nonsense.

Nico fumbled with his pants and then he shoved my dress up above my waist, pausing a minute to lift me onto the desk. Papers fluttered and pens tumbled to the floor, giving us away, but we didn't care. I spread my legs and he gently fished out the pleasure egg, tucking it away in his jacket pocket—our little secret.

Then he ravished my mouth as if he couldn't get enough. His tongue, his hands, all roving—tasting and touching—committing to memory every nook and cranny, every hill and valley.

We froze as voices sounded in the hallway, but they receded quickly and I smothered a relieved giggle. I couldn't imagine being caught like this would do Nico any favors when he was supposed to be here on an official capacity for his family business.

Impatient to be inside me, Nico pulled me from the desk and flipped me over to bend over the mahogany. The smooth wood beneath my cheek was cool as Nico gripped my hips and guided himself inside, pushing hard until he'd buried his shaft balls-deep. I groaned, losing myself to the pleasure of being taken like this, and wondered how I'd ever get over someone like Nico. How could anyone else possibly compare?

I groaned softly as he drove, sliding in and out with strong, controlled thrusts, building that beautiful tension like a master cellist slowly built to a crescendo. My fingers curled against the wood, my eyelids squeezing shut as I fought to keep the cry behind my teeth, but

Nico's name burst from my lips as I came, clenching and squeezing as every muscle contracted and released in perfect concert.

God, he could fuck.

I was dimly aware of Nico finding his own release, grinning with sated pleasure at how sexy he sounded when he came. There was something so primal about the act of climax that aroused me even as I was content to simply try to slow my thundering heart rate.

Nico withdrew and tossed the condom in the waste bin, then helped me from the desk. We dropped into a spacious divan and lay there in the milky dark, completely disheveled but entirely happy.

Moonlight shafted in through the expansive window and the stars punched diamond sparkles in the midnight tapestry. I didn't know whose office this was or how much trouble we'd be in if we were caught; all I knew was I didn't want this moment to end.

It felt like magic.

"You are the most beautiful woman in the world," Nico murmured, idly playing with an errant curl lazily tumbling down my shoulder. "I can't believe I ever thought you were plain."

I blushed at the memory of that first meeting. "I have a confession…"

I heard the smile in his tone as he said, "Yeah? Confess, my darling."

"I purposefully came to the interview wearing the ugliest dress I had. I knew of your reputation, but more so than that, Patrice had made a snide comment about my wardrobe, which she was doing constantly, and I think I did it out of spite. I know, stupid."

"Do you miss working at *Luxe*?" he asked.

I hesitated, giving the question serious thought. "I miss some of my coworkers, but I don't miss the bullshit. Publishing is a dog-eat-dog world. It's almost inevitable that you're going to get eaten or take a bite out of someone else at some point. I don't miss that part." I twisted around to meet his serious gaze, those eyes doing something dangerous to my insides, but I managed to stay focused. "We really need to do some work on your project. You hired me to do a job. I don't feel right accepting payment for work I haven't done yet. In fact, you should've only paid me half up front and the other half when I delivered."

"Screw the project," Nico said, yawning, and I frowned. *Screw the project?* Nico seemed to sense my sudden disquiet and he clarified, "I mean, screw the project right now. I don't want to talk work. I want to enjoy having the most incredible woman on my arm."

I relented—I mean, how could I not when he said things that made me melt?—saying, "Well, when you put it that way..." I brushed a soft kiss across his lips and he reciprocated. I smiled. "Thanks for tonight. It's been exquisite."

"The pleasure has been mine," he said, and while it could've sounded obligatory or trite under any other circumstances, I sensed that Nico meant every word.

Or maybe that was his gift—he could make a woman believe anything that fell from his lips.

"Nico...I'm curious...have you ever been in an actual relationship?" I asked.

He sighed. "Once, no, twice. Both times ended badly."

I bit my lip. I probably shouldn't have asked, but I needed to know if he was even capable of deep emotion or if I was seeing things that didn't exist when he looked at me.

"Tell me how you and Houston met," Nico said, expertly *defecting* as Grady would say.

"I was in college. We met at a party. We were both drunk. He was supposed to be a good time, not a long time, if you know what I mean. But he made me laugh. I was so stressed with midterms that I needed someone to shake things up, make me smile."

"I've never known Houston to be particularly funny," Nico said with a slight sniff, and I giggled at the obvious pinch of jealousy. "But then, I suppose your brain was starving for entertainment," he teased.

I laughed. "Yes, well, it was a perfect storm of bad judgment, and before I realized in time that it was time to cut my losses, I got pregnant."

"And Houston bailed when you told him?"

"Actually, he stuck around for a month or so but when things started to get real, he slowly stopped calling and coming around. Basically, he ghosted me." I realized something, laughing as I shared, "Come to think of it, I guess technically, we're still dating because we never broke up."

"You're definitely broken up," Nico growled, holding me more tightly. "He's a pussy for skipping out on his responsibility."

I recognized that tone and I tried to keep things light. I rose up and shimmied over his hips to straddle him, my fancy dress pooling around my hips as my hot folds rested on top of his quickly hardening cock.

"I don't want to talk about Houston," I said in a silky tone, sliding my pussy over his groin. "I want round two before we're discovered and thrown out for being disrespectful perverts."

"I've been called a pervert my entire life. I wear that badge with honor," Nico growled with a sexy smile tugging at his lips as he reached between us to push up inside me. I rode him slowly, lifting my hips and grinding, loving the way his hands anchored at my waist to guide and control my movements, his hooded gaze centered on the spot where our parts joined.

My name lingered on his gasped warning, and I smiled with anticipation at how well we meshed together sexually. I wanted to ride him to completion, but that wasn't wise.

I rose up and he pulled out with a small groan of disappointment until I replaced one hot, wet orifice with another. We were out of condoms and I wasn't going to risk pregnancy, but it was no tragedy to have Nico in my mouth. I loved his taste and I adored the taste of myself on his skin as I worked him without mercy.

He came with a loud grunt, filling my mouth, and I quickly swallowed, sucking every last drop down my throat, loving how easily I could turn this charming playboy into putty in my hands...er...mouth.

Finished, I wiped my mouth and smiled, though I realized, too late, Nico was going to be a hard habit to break. I helped Nico to his feet and he pulled his pants up and buckled them with an adorable grin that was both sexy and boyish, and I wanted to do even more wicked things together.

Hell, I'd be willing to do just about anything with Nico. Even butt stuff. And that was saying a lot because I'd tried anal sex once and swore to never do it again.

"Why did your relationships end?" I asked, unable to let it go. I needed to know if Nico was simply incapable of deep emotion with another human being. Why? Because a part of me was starting to hope that he felt the same way as me and that, maybe, *just maybe*, we might have something worth exploring.

But if I were spinning my wheels in mud, I needed to stop right now and save myself from drowning.

CHAPTER TWENTY-FOUR

Nico

I SENSED THE energy in the room change between us. Even though Lauren was trying to seem nonchalant about her probing question, I could sense that it was anything but lighthearted.

I knew I ought to play it off with some sort of teasing answer and distract her with something else—my mouth on hers, perhaps—but something compelled me to be honest.

Which, in my experience, was never a good thing.

"I...uh, well, I was an idiot."

"Most men are idiots," Lauren teased and I didn't disagree, but I think I excelled in making the worst possible decision in any given situation. She cocked her head with interest as she asked, "What did you do?"

I hesitated, torn between tossing a joke or going for the bald truth. I opted for truth even though I wouldn't come out looking so hot. "I cheated. Both times. It was hurtful and wrong, and I didn't have a solid good reason for what I'd done to either of them. Both were great women who didn't deserve how I hurt them."

A long pause stretched between us. I knew how

most women felt about "cheaters," and I didn't blame them. Hell, my brother's wife, Katherine, threatened to bail on a marriage contract that'd been in play since she was sixteen because she'd thought Luca had cheated on her.

It all came out in the wash that he hadn't—Luca wasn't that kind of guy to begin with and he'd been head over heels in love with Katherine since forever—but the hell she'd put him through to get to the aisle wasn't for the faint of heart.

Let me just say, there was a hostel and a soup kitchen involved.

"Were you sorry?" Lauren asked quietly, breaking into my thoughts. I didn't want her to think being genuinely contrite made any difference in the hurt I'd caused, but yeah, of course I'd been sorry.

"People caught red-handed doing something wrong are usually very sorry. Doesn't change what I did. Twice. Seems I have a thing about *not* learning from my past mistakes." I shrugged into my tuxedo jacket. "The thing is, I have this aversion to commitment, it seems. Just when things are going great, I have to go and do something awful to ruin it all. It's my MO, which is why I don't get into relationships anymore. Best to stay single. That way no one gets hurt."

Even though it was dark, I could sense Lauren's disquiet at my admission. I smothered the urge to smooth over my admission with a lie to preserve the sweetness between us, but I couldn't sully the first real thing I'd allowed myself to feel in years by being disingenuous.

"People make mistakes and they change and grow," Lauren said. "Or they don't and they keep making the same mistakes, but either way, it's their choice one way or another."

"Which is why you don't date anymore either because of Houston."

"I don't date because I have a sensitive six-year-old who is more important to me than the inconvenience of suffering a few nights of loneliness."

"Lauren, I was honest with you, do me the courtesy of being the same," I said, not letting her skate past without at least owning her actions, as well. "You're afraid of being hurt." Her silence confirmed my assumption and prompted me to admit, "Well, I am, too. I'm afraid of hurting another good woman."

A woman like you.

I didn't like how the mood had changed. The night, to this point, had been the most fantastic on record, and I hated how such serious talk had put a blemish on an otherwise perfect evening. I gathered Lauren in my arms, and she went willingly. I inhaled the sweet scent of her perfume and skin and committed it to memory. I knew this feeling and I knew to run from it before everything soured like milk left out in the hot sun.

Eventually, every relationship I was in curdled.

I wouldn't do that to Lauren and Grady.

Which meant I needed to either cut ties now and risk hurt feelings or finish my so-called project and end things on a professional note as agreed upon.

My inclination was to cut ties, but that would save only my feelings. Spending more time with Lauren and Grady, even under the guise of the project, would only prolong the inevitable and suck all of us deeper into quicksand.

I should've never interfered with Lauren's life. If

I hadn't barreled my way into her life, she would've been happy to go along as she always had, meting out a meager lifestyle on her paltry salary, but strong in her heart.

Now I was the thorn, burrowed deep, unwittingly killing her.

"We'll get started on the project tomorrow. Seriously."

She brightened, happy to be working again. "Awesome. I promise you won't regret hiring me. I can't wait to write your story. I'm going to make the world see the real you. *Including* your brothers."

Her genuine enthusiasm only made me feel wretched. The project had been a sham and my actions underhanded, but I had to see it through, even if I just stuck the finished manuscript in a box and lit it on fire. Dante was right; no one wanted to read about my life, what little I'd done with it.

But for now, I'd play the game for Lauren's sake because she deserved far better than having me crash into her life and ruin it.

I grasped her hand and asked with a rueful grin, "Shall we make our escape?" She nodded with a tremulous smile, and we slipped from the room to the exit where the car awaited.

CHAPTER TWENTY-FIVE

Lauren

NICO HAD ADMITTED the very thing I'd suspected all along—he was averse to commitment, which meant he wasn't the right fit for Grady and me.

His admission should've snapped me out of whatever spell Nico had been weaving around me, but it only served to make me want to cry. There was a side of him that was so incredibly sweet and generous, but maybe I was just falling for the charm and not the real Nico.

Who was the real Nico? I didn't know.

For that matter, I didn't know anything about him aside from that we were fantastic in bed together and my son thought he was better than sliced bread with peanut butter.

I didn't know his friends—aside from Houston, if Nico could call him that.

I didn't know his family—aside from that one awkward encounter with his brother Dante.

I didn't even know his favorite color.

Basically, I knew nothing because he never planned to make me a permanent part of his life.

To be fair, I'd known this from the start and supported it, but now the knowledge hurt.

Since it was late, I'd prearranged for Grady to stay the night with my mom, which meant I was free to sleep with Nico for the entire night if I chose.

But did I want to do that?

Probably not a good idea.

We arrived at the apartment—his place already felt like home—and just as I was about to turn toward the spare bedroom, Nico caught my hand and shook his head, that one wordless motion telling me everything I needed to know.

No words. No more conversation. Just our bodies doing what our bodies did best.

I closed my eyes as he undressed me with all the tender attention of a man who hadn't been with me only an hour prior, and I allowed the pleasure to roll over me as his tongue slipped between my folds to lick and suck until I broke out in a sweat and came hard.

Shuddering as the pleasure went bone-deep, I sighed as the last wave crashed over me, settling against Nico's naked body, limp and content.

And that was how I fell asleep.

The following morning I awoke before Nico. I rolled to my side and propped my head with my hand, smiling as he slept. He was the most beautiful man I'd ever seen. Truly. Almost too pretty. Between that wash of dark hair and those classic cheekbones, not to mention that killer body, he could give a Calvin Klein underwear model a run.

But from what I knew of the Donato men, they were all handsome. I could easily see how women wobbled to their knees whenever one was around.

All signs pointed toward walking away, cutting my losses, but when I looked at him, my heart did funny things and my lips wanted to smile, if only to give shape to the feeling in my soul.

As much as I liked to think I'd been in love with Houston…what I felt for Nico was nothing like how I'd felt about Houston.

This felt deeper, more stable and yet wildly intoxicating.

The way Nico was with Grady—there was no faking that emotion. He might be able to fool me, but whatever was happening between him and my son was 100 percent real.

And it was the same for Grady.

Damn it—I knew I shouldn't have let Grady get attached, but how could I not when Grady had been so happy?

Nico's eyes opened slowly and he graced me with a sleepy smile as he reached for me. "Stalker," he murmured. "Did you take pictures while I was sleeping, too?"

"Only a few for blackmail purposes later," I answered, giggling as he burrowed his face against the crook of my neck. "You should be worried. I caught you drooling."

"Ah, truly damaging, indeed." He kissed the back of my neck, sending goose bumps rioting down my skin. "And what other trouble have you been up to while I slept? Does it include breakfast?"

I laughed. "Yes, I made a full-course meal while you drooled. Are you nuts? Eat a bowl of cereal."

"Damn, the honeymoon is over," he drawled, and I laughed harder until his hand started to travel down my belly, then my breath caught and I bit my lip, anticipating his touch. "I can't seem to get enough of you," he admitted, his fingers lightly skimming the soft skin of my folds. "Are you a witch or something? I think you've dosed me with Love Potion No. 9."

I stilled, turning to him. "I might ask the same of you," I countered, dancing around the highly charged word floating between us. I'd fallen for him. I'd done the very thing I'd sworn I wouldn't. But how did Nico feel about me?

Was love even an option?

His brow lifted even as his fingers continued to lightly strum the sensitive skin. "There's definitely some voodoo going on," he said. "I think the only answer is to constantly fuck each other's brains out in order for the magic to wear off."

I laughed but I stilled his hand. "I'm not sure that will work. I think it would only make things worse."

"Well, it's worth a try," he said, rolling on top of me, and as much as I craved the pressure of his body pressing down on mine, I shook my head. He frowned. "Are you okay? What's wrong?"

"I can't think when you're on top of me and your cock is nudging between my thighs," I admitted, encouraging him to roll off, but he didn't see the appeal.

"Morning sex is good for clearing the mind," he said, but when he saw I wasn't kidding, he rolled off with a sigh. "I guess you could blow me and that would be okay."

I snorted and climbed from the bed, wrapping a silk robe around me. "We have work to do. I'm going to shower, eat some breakfast and then go get Grady. In the meantime, I suggest you do the same. I want to get some notes down while Grady is at school. I think

I could have a rough draft of notes compiled within a week if we buckle down. Sound good?"

Nico looked bored with that plan, but he didn't protest any further. "Yes, Mistress Hughes," he said, making a whip-cracking motion and sound. "Whatever you desire."

I laughed. "I desire a cup of coffee and a jelly doughnut. Can you make that happen?"

"Coffee, yes. Doughnut, no."

I winked. "Get moving, lazy bones," I said, and left him there on the bed with a raging boner.

CHAPTER TWENTY-SIX

Nico

IN HINDSIGHT IT was always easier to see when you should have taken a left instead of a right, but that was the beauty of hindsight—clarity.

I knew Lauren wanted to get started as soon as she returned, but I needed some advice and maybe an ass-kicking. I texted Lauren to let her know I had errands to run and I wouldn't be back to the apartment until later that afternoon, and then I headed to my brother Luca's house.

One of the concessions Katherine had insisted upon in order to marry my brother was that they would not live in the Donato mansion, even though it was big enough to house a football team comfortably. I didn't blame her—my mother ruled the mansion with an iron fist and it was her way or the highway. Not to mention it was just way too big. It was like living in a cavernous museum with a full-time staff and a controlling drill sergeant for a roommate.

Luca and Katherine had purchased a modest home near enough to our parents' place but far enough to create some distance when they needed space.

Katherine opened the door, her distended belly coming into view before she did. "You look ready to pop," I joked, but my observation wasn't appreciated and she responded with a scowl. *Note to self: pregnant women lose their sense of humor along with their waistline.* Of course, then I wondered how Lauren had weathered pregnancy and I had to school my thoughts away from that topic altogether because, oddly, my cock started to tingle at the thought of Lauren's body swelling with a kid. Notably, *my* kid, and that was a problem.

Katherine gestured toward Luca's office, stating, "He's in there," before waddling off in the opposite direction, her hand resting on the small of her back as if that would change the fact that she was practically tipping over.

I walked into the office and found my brother behind the desk, looking so much like a younger version of our father, Giovanni. Luca had always been our father's favorite, even though he had a funny way of showing it. Our father had never been the warm and cuddly type. Maybe that was why I had commitment issues. Though, to my knowledge, our father had never cheated on our mother. Giovanni was just an asshole. I honestly couldn't imagine anyone else wanting to sleep with him, because he was just unpleasant most days.

Not that you would know it by our mother. Our mother still thought he was handsome and virile. I suppose that was the way it was supposed to be. No matter what you looked like on the outside, your husband or wife should always have your back. I guess that was one lesson that our parents had succeeded in teaching.

Go, Team Donato.

I sank into the chair across from my brother with a loud sigh.

Luca smiled as he looked up from his computer. "Feeling a bit dramatic? What's the problem today?"

True, to this point my troubles had been small, but the weight of the world was resting on my shoulders, even though I'd pretty much put the weight there myself.

"How's married life? Katherine seems pretty grumpy. Are you already in the doghouse?" I asked, choosing not to jump right into my problem.

But Luca wasn't stupid. "You didn't really come over to talk about my pregnant wife, did you? That's not really your style."

Yeah, he was right. I was stalling. I leaned forward. "Here's the deal, withhold your judgment until I've finished telling my story," I warned. Luca nodded and I pressed forward. "I may have done something really stupid, and I don't know how to get myself out of it without hurting someone that I've come to care about."

That got his attention. "My little brother actually caring for someone? Surely that's a sign of the coming Apocalypse."

Ha, ha. "I'm being serious. I need your advice."

Luca sobered appropriately. "All right, I'm all ears. Lay it on me."

I didn't pull any punches or soften the truth. I told Luca everything from how I'd manipulated the situation to place Lauren in my debt as well as how I'd maneuvered her into my bed. I also admitted that I had feelings for her and for Grady.

Luca steepled his fingers in thought, his brow dipping as a subtle frown formed. He wasn't happy. I braced myself for the lecture I deserved. "Nico, when are you going to learn you have to stop fucking with people's heads?"

"That's just it, Luca. I think I..." The word stuck on my tongue, but I felt it in my heart and I just threw it out there. "Jesus, Luca, I think I love her."

"You *think*? If you have a question at the end of that statement, then you don't actually love her. Love is something that grabs you by the balls and doesn't let go. If you don't feel that emotion in your soul, it's not love and you need to let her go before things go south, fast."

Which was exactly what Dante had said in a different way. But, of course, Dante's biggest fear had been that my dalliances might somehow rebound on the family business.

More miserable than before, I said, "I know I should just let her go, but every time I think about saying the words I can't get them out. I mean, she's so great. Even if you took away all the physical attributes that I'm into, I'd still be over the moon about her. She's smart, talented and fucking funny as hell. And that kid of hers? He's bloody fantastic. I took them sailing the other day and it reminded me why I love sailing. I want to take Grady sailing every day because he loves it. I want to buy him his own damn sailboat. I'm having all sorts of dangerous thoughts, and I can't make them stop. Do you know where they live? In a shitty apartment in *Brooklyn* and I want to...hell, I want them to live with me forever. For real, not just temporarily."

Luca pumped his hands with a "Whoa, brother, calm down. You're dealing with emotions that you have no experience with. You can't handle people like Lauren and Grady with inexperienced hands. That kid isn't yours, and I'm not sure you're ready to be a father."

"I'd be a far better father than his actual dad. The loser just abandoned his own kid. What the fuck is that shit?"

"Not your problem," Luca reminded me in a stern tone. Then he added something else, "Think of how our parents would react to your bringing home a single mother with a kid. You know how Mom feels about those things. It's just best to cut ties cleanly and quickly before things get way too messy."

Of course, Luca was right. But it was the absolute last thing that I wanted to do. I wanted to do the opposite of Luca's advice. I wanted to, maybe, marry Lauren, and I said as much. "Yeah, well, what if I'm in love with Lauren and I wanted to marry her? Our parents would just have to deal with it."

Luca shook his head at my defiant statement. "That's your problem, little brother, you're always thinking of yourself and not how your actions affect others. Do you really think Lauren wants to be part of this family? Katherine's known us her entire life and she nearly couldn't marry me because of everything it entailed. What makes you think Lauren is going to want to jump into the chaos that is the Donato family?"

All valid points.

I didn't care.

"You'd like her."

Luca sighed, shaking his head. "Why'd you come over here to ask for advice you weren't going to take?"

"I think I love her. No, I do love her," I asserted, feeling stronger every second the more I allowed myself to say the words. "I want to marry her."

"You're getting ahead of yourself. You don't even know if she wants to marry you," Luca warned.

"Why wouldn't she?" I countered, feeling smug. If Luca knew how well I made her come, he wouldn't ask that question. If there was one area I felt 100 percent secure, it was in the bedroom. And there was no denying Lauren and I created sparks whenever we were near one another. "Yes, she'll want to marry me."

"Let's just pretend for a second that she's willing to marry you…is she still going to feel that way once she finds out how you manipulated her? In my experience, women tend to take a dim view on that sort of shit."

"I won't tell her and thus she'll never know," I said. "I'm sure there are things you've never told Katherine."

"If you take one bit of advice from me today I hope it's this…don't fucking lie to the woman you profess to love. Lies always manage to rise to the top, like a fucking body in a lake. There's no amount of cement that can keep the truth from popping up."

I shifted with unease. If Lauren found out about my involvement with her getting let go from *Luxe*, she'd never forgive me—that was a fact.

"If she finds out after we're married, she'll forgive me," I said, but Luca's expression just told me I sounded like an idiot.

Maybe I was, but I had to take that risk. Besides, what were the odds that Lauren would find out, anyway?

I grinned at Luca. "Guess I'd better make a stop at the jewelers. I have a purchase to make."

CHAPTER TWENTY-SEVEN

Lauren

I wasn't surprised Nico had texted to tell me our plans to work would have to wait for the time being. For someone who had hired me to do a job, he was fairly reluctant to actually sit down and get the project started.

I didn't mind the break, though. I managed to stop by my apartment and water my plants as well as check my mail. After shredding the junk and doing some general cleanup so the place wasn't a wreck when we returned, I grabbed some fresh clothes for both me and Grady and started to head back to Nico's until I decided to detour and pick up takeout from my favorite Americana restaurant.

Chester's was my and Grady's go-to spot for burgers and fries. I ordered and waited, stepping aside with my phone in hand, checking my emails for any word on the countless résumés I'd sent out.

But as I waited, a familiar voice at my back caused me to turn.

Patrice.

I forced a polite smile at the awkward encounter. I

hadn't realized Patrice was a fan of burgers—I'd always pictured her as more of a sushi and wheatgrass kind of person—but there she was, standing in all her pinched-expression glory, giving me the most condescending look I'd ever seen.

"How are you?" I asked, making conversation. "How is *Luxe*?"

"I wouldn't know. I was fired."

I tried not to let my jaw drop. "I'm so sorry. What happened?"

"As if you don't know," she returned with a sour expression that confused me. "Your boyfriend's little shenanigans cost me my job." She patted her hair as she drew herself up. "Thankfully, I have plenty of friends in this business and I was able to rebound. Unlike you, I'd dare say. How's the job hunting going?"

I narrowed my gaze. "What are you talking about?"

"After what your boyfriend pulled, you'll be lucky if you can find a job writing ad copy for dog food."

I was starting to fume, but I needed to know what the hell Patrice was talking about before I punched her in the nose. "I have no idea what you're talking about, but if you've been bad-mouthing me to prospective employers, I could sue you for defamation."

"I haven't said anything that wasn't true," Patrice said, undeterred. "And don't act so innocent. I'm sure you were well aware of what that asshole Donato was up to when he forced me to fire you."

The contents of my stomach dropped to my bowels. "What?" I could barely get the word out, my throat had closed so tightly. "I don't understand."

Patrice stared as if she didn't believe me, but when she realized I was genuinely floored, her expression turned sly and vindictive. "Trying to play the victim? How quaint. Donato came to me, promising advertising dollars for *Luxe* if I convinced you to attend the Griffin dinner with him. I tried, but you had other plans. I never imagined he'd pull his campaign because of something so silly, but he threatened to do just that, saying that if I didn't fire you that he'd pull every cent of a very lucrative deal that I'd already sent to advertising. Against my better judgment...I did it. Well, corporate caught wind of what'd happened and said I'd grossly abused my power and let me go."

I could only stare. I thought I was going to vomit.

Patrice sniffed. "But it seems you landed on your feet. Everyone saw you and Donato cuddled up at the Griffin dinner, looking like two lovesick puppies. *Luxe* got the advertising campaign, but I got the shaft. Seems everyone came out on top but me."

"I didn't have anything to do with Nico's...deception," I said, my eyes blurring. Nico had betrayed me in the worst way. I couldn't quite reconcile the facts when my heart was screaming.

"Well, you can kiss my ass for a good reference because I don't believe you."

I swallowed the lump in my throat. How could I be so stupid as to believe Nico was capable of anything genuine? Anything real?

Oh, God, and I'd exposed Grady to Nico's manipulation, as well. I didn't wait for my food and simply bolted.

Patrice's laughter seemed to follow me, or maybe it was just the voice in my head telling me I should've known better.

Either way, Grady and I weren't going to stay another minute in Nico's place.

In my current state of mind, I was afraid I might murder him.

CHAPTER TWENTY-EIGHT

Nico

EVERYTHING WAS READY. My hands were shaking, but my mind was made up.

"Marry me," I practiced in the mirror several times, thrusting the black jewelry box toward an imaginary and ecstatic Lauren.

"Lauren...will you please marry me?"

"Lauren...make me an honest man...marry me!"

"Will you freaking marry me, please?"

"Grady, can I marry your mom?"

I double-checked that I looked on point. I wanted to look my best for my future wife.

I shivered at the word *wife*. Who would've thought that Nico Donato could be tamed? I chuckled, feeling pretty proud of myself. I was already picturing our wedding. Of course, Grady would be my best man. I couldn't imagine anyone I would want more than Grady standing beside me as I married Lauren.

A contented sigh rattled free, and I checked my watch. Lauren should be here any minute.

As if on cue, the apartment door flew open and

Lauren came in, Grady in tow, but she was anything but smiling.

"Grady, pack your things," she said, her tone leaving no room for argument. Grady shot me a sad look that killed me, and I couldn't process what was happening fast enough.

"Whoa, what's going on?" I asked, chasing after Lauren as she started shoving clothes into her suitcase, ignoring me. "Lauren…what's wrong?"

"Mama said you did a bad thing…" Grady answered, sucking in his bottom lip to hide the tremble. "What did you do, Nico?"

A chill settled over me, but my skin felt damp. I swallowed, not quite sure how to answer. Surely she couldn't have found out about *Luxe*…was it possible Luca had sold me out? My world tilted and I searched for words. "Sweetheart—"

She whirled on me, her eyes blazing, "Don't you dare call me sweetheart or any word remotely attached to an endearment, or I swear I will split your skull open with this lamp."

Holy shit, she knew. How? "Let me explain," I said, forgoing any attempt at covering my tracks. It didn't matter how she knew. I had to fix things now or lose everything.

"There is nothing you could possibly say that would forgive what you did to me, Nico. You forced Patrice to fire me? So that you could…make me attend a dinner with you? What the fuck is wrong with you?"

"To be fair, if you hadn't turned Patrice down in the first place, none of this would've happened." *Ah, shit.* I knew the minute the words fell from my fool mouth they were the wrong thing to say. I stumbled on more words in my rush to pull my foot out of my mouth. "I was wrong to do what I did. All I can say is I'm sorry… I wasn't thinking of how that might end up, but things worked out for the better, right? I mean, there's no way you could've made it working at *Luxe* for much longer. Now you can afford to live somewhere nicer…somewhere—"

"I like where I live," she cut coldly, jerking her suitcase closed and zipping with a savage motion before going to Grady's and doing the same. Grady was crying quietly, and I wanted to die. Hell, how had things gone so sideways in such a short amount of time? "Lose my number," she said in a low tone that seethed with rage. "I fucking hate you."

I wanted to grab her and make her listen, but I knew I didn't have the right to touch her right now; plus, I was a little afraid she might actually make good on her threat and split my head open with the lamp.

"Grady…"

But they were gone, the door slamming behind them. The last image of Grady, tears running down his round cheeks from behind those owlish glasses, breaking my heart in two.

Holy fuck.

My entire world had just collapsed right at the moment I'd discovered what my entire world was made of.

I stared at the closed door, my heart thundering in my chest.

"I want to marry you, Lauren. Jesus…I'm sorry."

The ring box slipped from my fingers to drop to the floor.

What was I going to do?

How did I make this better? Was it even possible?

Or had I just lost the one woman who was made just for me over a dumbass move that I'd take back in a heartbeat if I could.

I was out of my depth, but I knew I needed to give Lauren some space, even though every nerve in my body was screaming at me to follow her and drag her back.

She just needed to go home and calm down, breathe and realize that I was sorry, and then she would forgive me and we would get back on track to bliss.

Yeah, solid plan. Except my heart was still skipping beats, my palms were sweaty and I felt like I needed to puke.

God, help me. I really fucked up this time.

CHAPTER TWENTY-NINE

Lauren

FOR THE FIFTH consecutive day, a huge, ostentatious flower arrangement arrived, and for the fifth consecutive time, I dumped it down the trash chute.

Grady, unusually quiet since leaving Nico's apartment, watched as I silently fumed at Nico's dogged refusal to leave us alone.

The calls and texts—I blocked.

The flowers—I trashed.

The voice mail on my home machine—I deleted.

Somehow, he even managed to find my email; I deleted that, too.

I didn't want anything to do with Nico. I was half tempted to donate the money he'd given me for the fake project to charity, but I needed money to live.

So, even though I hated it, I had to keep the cash, and that just pissed me off all over again.

True to Patrice's word, she'd trashed me around town. No one would hire me right now. Not even the small newspaper I'd contacted out of desperation.

At this point I'd happily take writing ad copy for dog food, but not even they were willing to hire me.

If Nico's project had been real I could've used it as a great springboard, but just like everything associated with Nico, it was fake and useless.

Each morning, I cried in the shower so Grady didn't see me break down, but sometimes I couldn't help myself and I found tears running down my cheeks.

Like right now.

"Mama?" Grady's worried voice ate at me. I wiped away the tears and tried to smile for his benefit. He crawled into my lap and I rested my chin on his little head. "Are you going to stay mad at Nico for a long time?"

I cursed his name inside my head, hurting for my son as much as I hurt for myself. "Probably," I answered truthfully.

"What if he said he's sorry?" Grady asked. "You said that saying sorry is the best thing to do when you've done something bad."

"Yes, but it doesn't always work that way with adults," I said, wishing I could erase Nico from Grady's memory. "Nico isn't going to be part of our lives anymore. We need to put him behind us and focus on moving forward."

But Grady wasn't interested in moving forward. "But I miss him."

"Eventually, you'll stop missing him," I assured my little guy, but I wasn't sure if that was true because there was a Nico-sized hole in my heart that I didn't think would ever heal. I wasn't going to pretend that Grady wasn't suffering the same pain. I could only hope that eventually Nico would fade away in both our memories.

Fat chance, but I could hope.

"What did he do?" Grady asked.

"Honey, it's grown-up stuff. I don't want to talk about it right now, okay?" I kissed his forehead and held him tight. "We don't need Nico anyway. We're a team, right?"

Grady nodded, but I felt his sadness weighing me down like a rock in my pocket.

"How about we order pizza and have a movie night?"

But Grady didn't want pizza or popcorn or even soda. He hated our apartment, wanted to go sailing and wanted to see Nico. Nothing I did was going to measure up, and I just had to weather his disappointment. I'd done the cruelest and most careless thing imaginable—I'd given my little son a glimpse of what it might be like to have a father and then I'd taken it all away with little explanation aside from "Nico did a bad thing." It was little wonder Grady was sullen, sad and angry.

And I didn't know what to do to fix things. I had a sinking feeling that only time would make things better, but that didn't do much for either of our broken hearts.

CHAPTER THIRTY

Nico

I'D NEVER EXPERIENCED the awful drag of time until a month had passed since Lauren left and I thought surely it'd been longer than thirty days.

My ragged heart felt as if it'd been chewed and spit out by a rabid dog and then shit on.

Against my better judgment, I agreed to accompany Dante to the club to hit a couple of balls at the driving range. Golf wasn't my usual go-to sport to let off some steam, but seeing as I'd been hibernating in my apartment, existing on takeout and ice cream, I didn't think I'd have the stamina for much else.

I'd even gained a few pounds.

"You need to hit the gym," Dante said with a grimace when I groaned to tie my shoes. "You look like you've gained twenty pounds."

"Fuck off," I muttered, breathing a little heavier as I stood up. "So I've gained a few pounds, big deal. I've been a little messed up."

"Don't be a pussy," Dante said as we walked into the country club, flashing a cool smile to everyone who made the effort to notice us. "You've been moping around in that apartment so much you've started to grow mold. Pick yourself up, shake it off and move on. Isn't that what you do best?"

Yeah, but I'd never been in love with any of the women I'd moved on from. Not the case with Lauren. I still dreamed about her, fantasized about her and missed her like a fat kid missed cake.

Except, according to Dante, I was becoming the fat kid.

"She won't accept any of my calls," I said, ignoring Dante's look of disgust. "I've had flowers delivered, but she throws them away. How do I know that? I paid the neighbor to tell me if she accepts or tosses them. She tosses them. Right down the garbage chute. I tried leaving a voice mail on her home phone, but she changed her number. Aside from stalking her—"

"Sounds like you're already doing that," Dante cut in drily. "Give it a rest. You sound pathetic."

"I love her," I said simply. "I can't give up."

"She's moved on. You need to, as well."

We got to the range and I started to grab my nine iron when I heard a familiar voice. I turned to see Houston Beaumont laughing it up with his buddies a few lanes down. I looked away, not wanting to see the man because I didn't trust my ability to remain calm when I was already unstable as fuck.

Living on Häagen-Dazs and Chinese food wasn't great for your mental health or your waistline, apparently.

My plan was to ignore him entirely but Houston saw us and headed over, completely unaware that I wanted to shove my nine iron so far up his ass the hosel of my club used his uvula as my tee.

"Holy crap, it's the Donato boys. I haven't seen you in ages. How the fuck are you?" Houston asked, clapping Dante on the back. "How's business?"

"Business is good," Dante answered, squinting against the sun. Houston had never been one of Dante's favorite people, but now he was Public Enemy No. 1 in my eyes.

Because I was already in a shitastic mood, I decided to poke the bear and see what happened.

"So, you have a kid…" I said, watching his reaction. "Never knew that until recently."

Dante narrowed his gaze and realized quickly enough where I was going with this. He cut his stare to Houston, and we were both suddenly judging him and Houston knew it.

"Uh, well, so she says," Houston tried joking, playing off my question. His buddies shifted nervously. I knew I had to be radiating rage, but I didn't care. I was so pissed off and mad at the world that I'd take the first sorry sap with the misfortune to cross me. It just so happened, fate was smiling at me and threw me a bone by putting Houston Beaumont in my path.

"You're a piece of shit," I said, my voice hard as steel. "Anyone who abandons their kid is an asshole."

"Hey, fuck you, you don't know my life. How the fuck was I even supposed to know if the kid was mine? I've seen pictures. He doesn't look anything like me. You know how girls like her are…the kid could've been anyone's."

Now he was calling Lauren a whore? I advanced toward Houston, my fists curled. "You're right, the boy doesn't look anything like you—that's a blessing— but I'd advise you to watch your mouth before it overloads your ass. You're five seconds away from getting my fist in it."

Houston scowled and bowed up on me, going toe-to-toe. "You seem to know a lot about business that doesn't concern you, Donato. Why don't you back the fuck up and stick your nose elsewhere."

"Lauren and Grady *are* my business," I growled. "You don't deserve to say their names, much less talk shit about them."

Houston looked to Dante for backup but Dante was enjoying the show, resting his arm on his driver, a cool smile on his face. Like I said, Dante had never been a Houston fan, not enough action to back up his running mouth.

"Yeah? Fuck you, Donato. You want to champion a slut who had the bad luck to get knocked up, go ahead…but step off before I fuck up your world."

That was all the invitation I needed. I reared back and popped Houston in the nose with a savage cross that sent blood spraying from his busted schnoz, and I took immense satisfaction in the gurgling howls as I dragged him up from the ground, my hands curling in his golf polo. "Don't you ever talk about Lauren, think about Lauren or even breathe in her direction, you hear me? Because if you do, I'm going to rearrange your fucking face so bad your own mother wouldn't recognize you. Understand?"

I shoved Houston into the arms of his buddies, and they dragged him off before I thought better of letting him go with only one punch. He'd need surgery to fix that nose if he didn't want to look like a boxer who went one too many rounds in the ring.

I shook my hand, flexing. Dante handed me the

cloth used to wipe down the clubs, and I cleaned off the blood from my knuckles. "Feel better?" he asked drily.

"Yeah, a little."

Dante sighed. "You know he's going to sue for assault."

"Let him." I didn't care. Hell, I didn't care about much. "That fucker abandoned Lauren and Grady. He hasn't paid a single penny toward Grady's support and Lauren has shouldered the responsibility all on her own."

"Since when did you become the champion of single mothers?" Dante's brow rose with sardonic amusement, but I didn't dignify the question with an answer. He knew it had everything to do with Lauren, not the fact that she was a single mom. Dante shook his head with mild annoyance. "Either go fix this situation or let it go. You can't go popping people in the face every time someone pushes your buttons about Lauren."

"Haven't you been listening? She won't take my calls, emails or texts. She returns every gift, throws away the flowers. What the hell am I supposed to do? Toss her over my shoulder and drag her to my place?"

Dante exhaled with irritation as if I were being deliberately stupid before saying, "If you want to win her back you have to figure out why she's this upset in the first place. Is it truly because you manipulated her out of a shitty job and paid her an exorbitant fee for a fake project? Something tells me she could get over that. What's really the problem? Dig a little deeper. The answer is staring you in the face."

I scowled at Dante, irritated and frustrated that my brother seemed to know the answer but was making me work for it.

But Dante was right. I didn't think the real issue was the job. Sure, she was pissed as hell, but she'd get over that eventually. An image of Grady's stricken expression, tears tracking down his face, blazed across my brain, and I knew there was only one thing that Lauren would never forgive—someone hurting her son.

And I'd hurt Grady by not being honest. I should've come clean with Lauren about the project and my hand in her lost position. I would've eaten all the crow she demanded, but I know I could've won her back. Grady never would've had to know, and right now, I know Lauren would've been wearing my ring.

Grady would've become my son.

My son.

The words hit me hard. The weight of such responsibility should've crushed me, but it felt amazing. I wanted to be Grady's father.

I wanted to be Lauren's husband.

More than anything.

And I meant all the way—not just because I wanted to marry his mama.

I wanted Grady to be a Donato.

I met my brother's gaze. "I need to talk to a lawyer."

Dante smiled, testing out his driver with a slow swing as he said, "Hope it works out for you, little brother," and I left the range.

I was sending all the wrong gifts, completely missing the one thing Lauren and Grady wanted.

A family.

Well, hot damn, that was what they were going to get.

CHAPTER THIRTY-ONE

Lauren

I WAS JUST settling in for the night. Grady was tucked against my side, the television on, but I wasn't actually watching anything in particular while Grady played a game on his phone.

I knew getting over a broken heart took time, but why did every minute seem more agonizing than the last? Nico had somehow burrowed his way into my heart in record time, and I was both irritated and flabbergasted at how I could love him so deeply when we still barely knew each other.

I never did find out his favorite color.

Or his middle name.

Or what his pet peeves were.

I knew his secret tickle spots and how to make him laugh. I knew that he snored lightly when he was in a deep sleep. I knew that he loved to cook and took pride in his culinary talents.

But all of that was surface stuff.

I hadn't known how cruelly he could twist the knife in my back or how easily he could ruin lives without forethought.

According to Ronnie, I was being ridiculous.

"Honestly, his methods were unorthodox, but he did you a favor getting you out of *Luxe*. You were in a rut, girlfriend" had been Ronnie's take on the whole sordid mess. Even if I could forgive Nico for manipulating a situation for his own gain, I couldn't forget how crushed Grady had been when everything fell to crap.

Maybe if Nico had been honest…maybe it wouldn't have mattered. Wasting energy on wondering was stupid and an exercise in emotional agony.

I had to move on, not only for my sake but for Grady's.

I withheld a sad sigh, not wanting to worry my little guy. Since moving out of Nico's, he'd been withdrawn and his eyes had lost that sweet spark that'd always melted my heart.

I knew he was brokenhearted, too, and that killed me.

Mom guilt, in all its varying shapes and sizes, was enough to cripple a rhino. I'd give anything to take it all back so my son didn't end up hurt.

I startled at the knock on the door. It was too late for visitors. Suddenly, all the complaints and concerns Nico had expressed about my apartment came flooding to me in a panic. I didn't have anything in the way of a weapon unless you could count my sharp wit. "Grady, go to your room," I told Grady, helping him up. I waited until he was safely in his bedroom before going to the door, grabbing a heavy candelabra to use as a bat if need be. "Who is it?"

A pause long enough to stop my heart and create visions of my own death at the hands of a psycho followed until I heard, "It's me, Nico."

And then my heart rate sped up like I'd just smoked

crack. "What do you want?" I asked, my voice catching and betraying my hurt and hope in the same breath. "Go away."

"May I come in? I have something for you."

"There's nothing you have that I want."

"Please."

It was the humble plea that broke me. Nico wasn't blustering or trying to be charming. He was simply asking in the most sincere way possible if he could come in for a moment.

I shouldn't let him in.

I should tell him to get the hell out.

But I didn't—I couldn't.

The truth was, I missed him.

I slowly unlocked the door and stepped away so he could come in. My breath caught. He looked as if he hadn't slept in weeks. His cheeks were puffy and... was that a little belly?

Had he been mainlining jelly doughnuts this whole time? Somehow the fact that our separation had affected him so viscerally made me tremble all the harder because there was no faking his pain.

I closed the door, locking it, but I cast a nervous glance toward Grady's bedroom, afraid of Grady's reaction to Nico's showing up. I was grateful when Grady remained in his bedroom but I knew he wouldn't stay there for long, so I needed Nico to get to the point.

"What do you want?" I asked, folding my arms across my chest.

Nico held a manila envelope in his hand. I caught a subtle shake as he handed me the envelope. "This is for you and Grady."

I frowned, confused. "What is this?"

"Just open it. You'll see."

Was this some sort of gimmick? Another fake project? I sighed and decided to humor him just so he'd leave. I opened the envelope and pulled a sheaf of legal paperwork. I frowned, even more confused when I saw Grady's name on the documents.

"What is this?" I repeated, my palms becoming sweaty. I saw Houston's name, and my vision blurred. This couldn't be what I thought it was. My gaze flew to Nico's, needing confirmation before I started crying. "Nico...what am I looking at?"

"Houston Beaumont has relinquished his parental rights to Grady. You'll never have to worry about him showing up on a whim, using his family money and influence to force visitation. Grady is yours and yours alone."

I'd never dared to dream that Houston would sign away his rights. It was what I'd always wanted but had been too afraid to push out of fear that Houston might retaliate and insist on being a part of Grady's life. I bit my lip, unable to stop the tears. I clutched the paperwork to my chest, unable to form words, so overwhelmed by the treasure in my hand. "How did you do this?"

"I convinced him that it was in his best interest to leave you and Grady alone. After a short conversation, he agreed."

I shook my head, confused and stunned. "Just like that? A conversation?"

"Well, I punched him in the face first, but after that, he seemed more than willing to walk away."

Nico had punched Houston. *In the face.* I smothered my watery laugh behind my hand. God, how many times had I wished I could do exactly that? But Nico had somehow made the impossible happen. I stared at the paperwork again, afraid I was dreaming or lying in a coma somewhere, hallucinating.

"This is real, right?" I couldn't help myself. "This isn't a joke or some kind of scheme?"

"I wouldn't joke about this. It's one hundred percent legal and binding, so I hope it's what you really want."

"God, yes," I exclaimed, holding the paperwork tightly. *Thank you* seemed so inadequate a statement for what I was feeling in my soul, but I said it anyway. "I'm so incredibly grateful. Thank you." Tears dribbled down my cheeks as I met his gaze, questioning. "But why? Why would you do this for us?"

Nico drew himself up with a deep breath, and I'd never seen him appear so vulnerable or scared. He swallowed, wetting his bottom lip, before answering humbly, "Because I couldn't make Grady *my* son until Houston was out of the picture." I gasped, my breath hitching in my chest as I shook my head, more tears coming. Was he actually asking if… Was this happening? Nico slowly went down on one knee, producing a black jewelry box, and I nearly fainted.

"Marry me, Lauren."

One simple statement held such power and depth—the power to make or break three separate lives.

He opened the box, and the prettiest diamond engagement ring twinkled in the light. "Nico…" I whispered, shaking my head. I couldn't see straight. My nerves were raw. "I…I…"

But then Grady burst from the bedroom, clearly listening to everything we'd been saying, and he was suddenly wrapped around me like a monkey, jabbering, "Say yes, Mama! Say yes! *Pllllease!*"

My heart sang through the sheen of tears that washed away the pain of the last wretched month, but I couldn't get my mouth to work. My throat had closed, and each time I tried to open my mouth, all I could do was gape like a fish and cry.

"Is that a yes?" Nico asked, peering up at me, his blue eyes worried.

I bobbed my head in a desperate motion, saying yes with my heart. Nico jumped up and placed the ring on my finger, still shaking, then sealed his mouth to mine, his joy and relief an echo of my own. I tasted his tears and mine. Forehead to forehead, he murmured with the utmost sincerity, "Thank God. I can't live without you, Lauren. I'm a lost soul and a pitiful bastard without you in my life." He drew a shuddering breath as he vowed fervently, "I promise to work every day to be the man you and Grady deserve."

I wanted to shout to the rooftops that he already was. Still clutching the paperwork to my chest, I watched as Nico then dropped down to Grady's level and said with the seriousness the occasion warranted, "Will you be my son, Grady Hughes? Will you do me the honor of becoming Grady Donato?"

Grady's little eyes welled with tears but he nodded vigorously in answer, and Nico folded him in his arms as if he'd always belonged there.

I couldn't love Nico more than I did in this moment. Everything else faded until it was only the three of us who existed in this world.

I knew he wasn't perfect, that he'd made mistakes

and would likely make more, but Nico loved us with a pure heart, and for that, I loved him all the more.

And in the warm space of that love, I forgave him for all the stupid crap he'd done before this moment.

Nico rose, hoisting Grady up with him, pulling me in for a deep kiss. In his kiss, I tasted love, commitment, laughter and joy—and I knew I'd finally found what I never knew I'd been searching for.

Nico was my soul mate, my touchstone, the future father to all my children and the man I couldn't wait to start a life with.

Even if I still didn't know his favorite color.

* * * * *

COMING SOON!

We really hope you enjoyed reading this book. If you're looking for more romance, be sure to head to the shops when new books are available on

Thursday
23rd August

To see which titles are coming soon, please visit
millsandboon.co.uk

LET'S TALK
Romance

For exclusive extracts, competitions
and special offers, find us online:

f facebook.com/millsandboon

@ @millsandboonuk

🐦 @millsandboon

Or get in touch on 0844 844 1351*

For all the latest titles coming soon, visit
millsandboon.co.uk/nextmonth